THE RESTAURANT BY THE COVE

ELLEN JOY

To my parents, who sparked my love for reading and writing.

Click HERE or visit ellenjoyauthor.com for more information about Ellen Joy's other books.

Beach Rose Secrets

CHAPTER 1

*R*achael laid all the money she could afford for a ticket on the counter. "One way to Camden Cove."

The gentleman behind the dividing glass dragged the cash underneath and counted it out, his attention on the computer screen. "Want a receipt?"

"No thanks." She adjusted her baseball cap as far down as possible, looking over her shoulder.

Then he looked up. It only took a second for his expression to change. He squinted to get a better look at her freshly swollen black eye. She eyed him back, challenging his stare, which made him look away. She'd put on her sunglasses, even if they hurt her face.

He slid over her ticket and she swiped it up without another word. With her sunglasses back on, she walked to the bus terminal. She'd wear them the whole rest of the ride, even as the sky darkened from the storm brewing over the city.

With each step, she checked behind her looking for Nick, trying to find his face among the crowd. Could he be out there? She knew he'd come looking for her as soon as he figured out she left.

As she climbed on board, she held her face low. She walked

down the aisle and took a seat in the back, then scanned the view out the nearest window.

Outside, the clouds swept across the sky as the wind picked up, stirring the sediments along the ground up into the air. A flag whipped its rope against a metal pole in a fitful, dinging rhythm. Rachael's heart pounded as though it was trying to break out of her chest.

"Start the bus," she whispered under her breath. Weren't they supposed to be leaving by now? An elderly woman boarded, stepping down the aisle and taking a seat three rows in front of her. A few more passengers climbed aboard.

From the corner of her eye, she saw a uniformed police officer walk down the bus terminal. She tilted her head down, pretending to look at her phone, but kept her good eye on him. He walked along the row of buses, hands resting on his belt. Her phone trembled in her hands as her throat dried up. Her head throbbed with her racing heartbeat.

"Let's *go*." The words growled out of her. A heavyset man in the bus company's uniform climbed the steps and sunk into the driver's seat as he closed the door. Was that police officer looking at her?

Once they hit the highway, the skies opened up and rain pounded down. Signs blurred by her for the first hour or so. It continued all the way through New Hampshire and obscured a glimpse of the Atlantic Ocean. A dense fog covered most of the water in a veil of gray.

The bus practically emptied out after stopping in Portland, and after a few more towns along the way, only Rachael remained. This far north, Rachael's TracFone couldn't pick up a decent signal. Her plans may have hit a speed bump, but Rachael would make do. She'd have to.

The pounding rain lulled her to sleep, but once her eyes slipped closed, Nick's face flashed in her head, startling her awake. With her jacket sleeve, she wiped the fog off the window. A "Welcome to Camden Cove" sign passed by as the bus pulled into a small station. Even in the rain, the seaside town looked the way she remembered. Quaint shingled buildings lined the street, with touristy shops only found next to the ocean. On a clear day, the view would be magnificent. But she hadn't really come to this tiny seaside town in the middle of nowhere for its views.

She gathered her things as the engine hissed to a stop, popping out of her seat.

"Visiting?" The driver stood at the driver's seat, waiting for her as she walked down the aisle.

She nodded, throwing her backpack over her shoulders.

"Hope you booked a place to stay for the night. Most places up here close during the off season."

"Thanks for the tip." She kept her eyes on the ground as she passed by him, descending the stairs. "Where could I grab a bite to eat?"

"There's few places down Harbor Lane. You'll want to take a right when you go out of the station, then swing a left on Main Street." He followed her out. "Tell them Phil sent you."

"Will do." She made sure to only show her good side.

Walking out of the bus station, she stopped at the corner of the street. Her empty stomach rumbled from the mention of food. When was the last time she had eaten? A place to sit down and figure things out sounded perfect right then. She protectively rubbed the wallet she had tied around her waist underneath her shirt. Her whole life savings, dangerously open to the world.

The streets were practically empty as she ran through the puddles trying to find anything that looked open. Did Phil tell her left, or right? Where were all the restaurants and hotels the website promised?

She wished she remembered where the tavern was located. Finn's Tavern would be open, but she wasn't ready to go there. Not yet.

Soon, she came across a parking lot with cars parked in front of a restaurant that had lights on — The Fish Market. But even from the outside, she knew the brown-shingled building wasn't a place she could afford on her very limited budget. There had to be a better option. Anything. But the rain made visibility poor, and from where she stood, nothing else seemed open. The whole town appeared deserted.

They had to have at least a soup she could afford. She hesitated, but for only a second. It was warmer and drier in there than out here in the icy autumn rain that fell in sheets, soaking her to the bone.

As soon as she stepped inside, the warm air wrapped around her like a plush blanket. She pulled off her hood and noticed a puddle forming on the floor underneath her. Scanning the room, the whole restaurant faced a man standing on top of a bench, giving a toast.

Oh, God. Was it a wedding?

Strands of wet hair clung to her face. She wiped it away from her eyes and saw the whole place hanging on the man's words. They all laughed at the same moment, and the woman next to him dabbed a tissue at her eyes. A beautiful bride embraced a happy groom.

It *was* a wedding.

Just as she felt her fingers again, she noticed a very attractive man staring at her. His eyes held a warmth that broke her chill.

From behind, someone tapped her on the shoulder. She spun around to see a boy in his teens. He pointed to a closed sign she had just caught sight of. "Excuse me, ma'am, but we're closed."

"Oh, the wedding," she moaned, and looked out the window to the dark, wet, night. "Is there any other place close by?"

She doubted it.

Oh, god, the man with the eyes moved his way toward her. Why did he look angry?

Jack Williams stood at the back of the dining room and just watched the crowd. He had everything under control. The whole event had gone off without a hitch. His sister and new brother-in-law had been completely happy with the impromptu location at his restaurant. The tropical storm brought heavy rains which ruined their plans for an outdoor wedding, but he had impressed the crowd, nonetheless.

His sister, Elizabeth, glowed as she walked around the room, greeting guests. She'd wave, then squeal and hug each person as her new husband, Adam, followed behind. Adam's daughter, Lucy, ran around the room and told stories of the animals on the farm where they all lived happily together.

It was enough to make someone believe in true love.

A half laugh escaped him as he glanced at his brother Matt sitting with his wife, Justine. He still needed to get used to the fact that those two were married. He looked away as soon as Justine snuck a glance toward him, walking away before any contact was made. He decided on a new location to observe the festivities away from his sister-in-law.

White linen covered all the tables, with bouquets of sunflowers, brown-eyed Susans and chrysanthemums. Decorative gourds scattered the tables around framed photographs of the couple. His sister Lauren and mom had spent hours decorating the place, going through old family photo albums of Elizabeth and the family, and asking Adam's family to do the same. Jack had thought they'd overdone it with all the time and effort they had put in, but he now admitted that people enjoyed seeing the images. Of course, they messed with Elizabeth and had secretly moved all the awkward teenage pictures of her in braces to the wedding party's table. His little sister didn't seem to enjoy it as much as they did.

"Seriously, you guys?" she rolled her eyes as Adam told her how beautiful she looked.

They were *that* annoying couple.

"Is the dessert ready to go?" His mother, Sarah, snuck up beside him. She couldn't control herself, he thought, reminding himself of how helpful she could be, even with all her overbearing tendencies. His parents had retired, and left the family restaurant to him, but they never quite took the plunge. He loved them. He really did. But he had moved back to Camden Cove to run the restaurant, not to have his mom looking over his shoulder while he made dinners.

"Everything's all set." He guided his mother back toward the dining room. "Go back and enjoy your daughter's wedding."

"Do you have the gluten-free cupcakes for your cousin Joey's son?"

"Yes, of course."

She rattled off another few questions as he steered her through the tables. Busboys cleaned up the finished plates of cake, and the servers refilled drinks. She knew the dinner had been a success. She just couldn't control herself.

Jack had outdone himself by creating an updated version of a traditional New England dinner. Instead of bland haddock, he had lobster served with a creamy lemon-herb butter sauce over fresh pasta. Filet mignon from local beef replaced the usual slab of prime rib. Jack spiced up the sedate flavors common in New England food with just the right twist, creating meals rivaling any featured in big-city restaurants.

Jack's natural talent in the kitchen was the reason why the restaurant had become a landmark in the small seaside harbor town. Not that his parents hadn't done well with the family business, but they certainly didn't bring it to the level he had. He was the reason people drove up from the city to dine in the restaurant everyone was talking about. He enjoyed the success, but he knew better than anyone how finicky the restaurant business could be.

He had grown up in this business, watching his parents run the restaurant. They worked their butts off to keep it a success, year after year, but they weren't willing to take risks. He was. He didn't have four children. In fact, he didn't have time to even imagine a family.

After dessert was served and the drinks refilled, John Williams, patriarch of the family, stood on a bench along the windows, delighting the crowd. The guests immediately took their silverware and clinked their glasses. His sister kissed Adam.

His father held up his drink toward Adam and Elizabeth, who beamed below him. His sister had never looked so happy. She looked stunning as a bride. And Adam wasn't such a bad guy. When he had heard about the newcomer he had been apprehensive, but he turned out to be a great fit for the family.

From beside him, Matt handed Jack a frosted glass of pale ale. "Another one bites the dust."

"Tell me about it." Jack shook his head at the thought of his baby sister Lauren getting married someday. "The lobsters were great."

His brother, the fisherman, along with his cousins, had supplied all the lobster for the night.

"Any time, brother." Matt slapped him on the back and toasted Jack's glass. He took a sip of his beer and leaned against the bar. "So, we're drinking to…?"

"Love, or maybe sacrifice?"

"Our Elizabeth," Matt whispered, as John started his speech.

"Do you want to get drunk?" Jack shook his head.

"Thirty-five years ago, when I first met Sarah, little did I know how much my life was about to change." John captured the audience.

"Family," Lauren said. The youngest Williams wedged her way through the crowd to the bar with her siblings. The traditional drinking game had started long before both girls were of legal age, one Christmas Eve when their dad gave a particularly long speech. Now whenever John got up to talk, which happened at most family events, they would choose a word.

"That's a good one," Matt said.

"Matt!" Justine hissed from their table. "Are you coming back?"

Jack swore Justine could freeze someone with just one look.

Matt faced Jack and rolled his eyes, but grabbed his drink to go. "Family, right?"

"Family," Jack repeated. He was annoyed with Justine, but she was Matt's problem now, not his.

"I never thought about the future until that moment, and even then, I hardly thought about having a family." John rambled on as the three Williams siblings took a drink. "But the night we had our first child, Jack, I realized I had better start. And so we did all the right things. We started saving for college and bought a house. We took out life insurance. Soon, there was Matt, and more planning. But it wasn't until Elizabeth was born that something about that future frightened me more than anything else in my life. And no matter how much planning I did, I would never be prepared for it. The day I would have to walk her down the aisle and give her away." He paused, choking up. The crowd made an, "ahh" which John countered with, "I'm not crying." The crowd laughed, and he returned to his story. "How could I ever give her to another? Who would ever love her more than Sarah and I? Would they cherish the simple things in life together? Or complicate things, like it's so easy to do? Would they understand the importance of family?"

They drank again.

"And would this man take care of Sarah and I in our old age?" He winked at Adam, making the crowd laugh again. "For thirty years, I have been praying this day would never have to come." Their father took a dramatic pause. "But in the end, I didn't have to worry about a thing. Sarah and I may have given our daughter away today, but we gained a son and granddaughter in return."

John took a breath as the crowd watched the happy couple, and lifted his drink to the crowd. "To family!"

"To family!" the crowd echoed, as the three Williams siblings all tapped their glasses together and took another drink.

Jack finished the rest of his beer. As his father continued on, the bell on the restaurant's front door jingled. Had he forgotten to put up the closed sign?

Over in the lobby, a woman stood dripping from head to toe onto his newly refurbished wood floor. At first, he was amused by the dripping-wet woman, as if she had stepped out of a comedy sketch. Then completely annoyed that she continued to stand there, dripping water all over the floors, until she looked up, her eyes wide like a deer caught in headlights.

One of the busboys gestured toward the closed sign, but the woman looked exhausted, and cold, and her hood did little to keep the wetness out. Her clothes were soaked through. He couldn't make out what she was saying, but the kid shook his head, gesturing to the dining room, following Jack's orders to keep out the public. But he hadn't meant to push a poor woman back onto the street in a storm. He left the reception as his dad continued talking about the early years at the restaurant, and walked over.

"Hold up, Cody," Jack said as he came up behind the waiter. "Excuse me, is there something I can help you with tonight?"

The woman looked up at him. Her face caught the light, and that's when he saw her eye. He almost reached out when he noticed the bruise ran down side of her face. "Are you okay?"

Her face fell and his heart with it. "I was just looking for a place to eat. I didn't mean to interrupt the wedding. I should leave." She turned around abruptly, but her feet slipped out from under her on the wet floor, and she fell backward.

Jack rushed in, grabbing her just in time before she hit the floor, holding her in his arms. She trembled, but before he could help her up, she pulled herself out of his grasp and stepped away from him.

"Thanks," she said, her voice barely audible.

Jack stepped closer to her. He hadn't seen a welt like that since senior year on Brian Devine when he got kicked in the face by his family's donkey.

Thunder rumbled outside. "Do you need help? Did you get in an accident?"

"I'm fine." She lifted her hand, covering her eye, using her coat sleeve as a shield. "I'll be out of your way."

An urge washed over him to wrap his arms around her to stop

her shivering. But her eyes had a storm brewing, bigger than the one outside.

She reached for the door handle and Jack sputtered out, "You can grab something to eat here, if you'd like?" She stopped, but kept her hand on the door handle. "I've got plenty of extra plates, unless you don't like lobster."

She didn't look at him as she spoke. "I'm afraid I can't afford a place like this."

"It's no problem. Come in and at least dry off before going back out there," he offered, hoping she'd stay. "There's a place where my staff takes their breaks, where you can eat alone. The food's just going to go to waste, anyways."

"I'm not broke. I just wasn't planning on having a lobster course." She kept her gaze low.

"Seriously, come in. Don't go back out there."

She hesitated, but stepped further inside. He put his hand on the back of her wet coat, and he felt her twitch as she moved forward, out of his reach.

He led her up the stairs to the loft area, where private dinners were held. Romantic dates, business ventures, and proposals all happened right there, overlooking the water. He grabbed a set of linens and silverware for the table, setting it as she sat.

"Seriously, you don't have to do this. I can just go to another place." She looked around. "It looks like you're sort of busy."

He smiled at her. "It's not a problem."

She looked over the railing of the balcony. "That's a big wedding."

"It's my sister's wedding."

"Oh, wow." She stretched her neck to see further.

"Would you believe it was originally a four-hundred-person guest list? My little sister was in charge of the invitations, and didn't want to exclude *anybody*."

He wasn't sure, but he thought he had seen a slight smile.

He set down a knife and fork and held out his hand. "I'm Jack."

She didn't extend hers at first, but eventually pulled it out from underneath the bag that sat on her lap. Her hand felt like ice, and although it still trembled, her grip was firm. When she let go, she stuffed it under the bag again. He waited for her to offer her name, but when she didn't, he didn't push it.

"Right, well, I'll be back with something from the kitchen."

"Thanks. Really." Her eyes flickered with sincerity and a bit of sadness, before she looked out over the railing again.

He raced to the kitchen to throw another plate together, suddenly wanting to know her name more than anything else in the world.

Rachael felt him checking her bruise, but not in a curious way like the guy at the bus station, but more in a concerned way, like a doctor examining a patient. But concerned or not, she didn't want him to scrutinize her face. The smart thing to do would be to leave, but she was so cold, and he was so kind. Something about him made her want to stay.

The man was definitely handsome, in the classic dark and mysterious mold. As nice as he seemed, he probably was just like most of the other men she had known in her life. And the last thing she needed in her life was another man. Even her father couldn't control his anger. How many nights did she hide under her covers, praying his rage wouldn't be turned on her? How many times did the police get involved, only to send him right back home?

How had she not seen it? How did she let down her guard and trust him? The badge, she thought, proved he was one of the good guys.

Nick's face flashed in her head.

"You alright?" Jack stood behind her setting down a tray on a table.

She shook her head to dispel the nightmare. "Yes, sorry."

He set a bowl of soup in front of her, then a breadbasket with a glass container of whipped butter. He filled one glass with water, and another with white wine. All the while, he was definitely laying on the charm. Maybe back in the day that kind of thing would've worked on her, but not any longer.

"Really, this is too much." His generosity *was* too much, there had to be a catch. She was betting this kind of restaurant didn't take just anybody off the streets.

"It's not a problem." He stuffed the tray under his arm. "You're not from around here, are you?"

She didn't respond, but her coolness didn't deter him.

"Are you staying in town?"

"Yes."

"It's pretty slim pickings, this time of year. Do you have a reservation somewhere?"

Was desperation written on her forehead? Then, the throbbing on the side of her face reminded her.

"I've booked something."

A growl came from her stomach, so loud she swore the whole restaurant could hear.

He smiled. "I'll let you eat."

Alone again, her shoulders relaxed a bit, and she grabbed the linen napkin to try to pat dry some of the wetness. Giving up, she grabbed a roll and pulled it apart. Steam rose from the center as she dipped a piece into the rich, creamy soup. Immediately, her body warmed as she tasted the chowder. Maybe it was because she was so hungry, or maybe it was because she was so cold, but the soup was the best thing she had ever eaten.

Rachael grabbed the glass of wine and took a big gulp. The light citrusy flavor was something she would've chosen when she enjoyed cooking for Nick. When things were good between them. When he enjoyed her company, and when her mistakes, or a bad day, didn't end in an eruption of emotions.

With the last of the bread, she wiped off the remaining soup and heard the sound of climbing footsteps. Jack appeared with two plates in his hands.

"I wasn't sure what you might like, so I brought it all."

He set two steaming dishes on another table, then cleared her bowl and bread plate away. With a flourish, he presented the entrees.

"This looks amazing." It was more like someone's idea of a last meal for the condemned, than a quick bite for someone who just stepped in off the street. His generosity made her feel vulnerable and she didn't like it. "Thank you."

"My pleasure," he said. "I think I missed your name."

The voice inside her head said not to tell him. To be suspicious, even if his behavior seemed innocent. But something about him made her trust him.

"I'm Rachael."

CHAPTER 2

"*H*ow many nights can I pay ahead?" Rachael didn't know why she asked the man behind the check-in counter at the inn. She didn't know how long she planned to stay in the deserted town.

"Well, you can pay up to the end of the month, but we're closing for the season after that."

"That's Thursday." Finding a place to rent within that time-frame seemed next to impossible.

"Yes, ma'am." The man clicked the computer keys with his index fingers.

"Oh." She opened her wallet, pulling out cash. "I'll take the room until then."

He opened the register. "There's a complimentary continental breakfast in the morning." He passed her a folder with brochures stuffed inside, along with a plastic hotel key. Thank God the hotel had off-season rates. Otherwise, she might have seriously slept on the streets.

For the millionth time, she second-guessed her decision to leave. Could she really run away? Was Camden Cove far enough? It was all she had. She squeezed the folder and headed to her room. She'd just have to figure out a way.

She turned the shower on when she got inside the room, turning the water pressure all the way up. She held her hands under the flow, feeling the temperature slowly rise. Her fingers were still frozen.

She left the water running and back into the room, keeping the lights off. Throwing her bag on the bed, she walked to the sliding glass door and pulled it open. Even through the rain, she could hear the waves off in the distance, crashing against the granite cliffs.

For a fleeting moment, she felt free.

The feeling disappeared as quickly as it came, as though whisked away by a thief. Freedom was gone, replaced with trepidation.

Steam escaped the bathroom when she walked back in. She could barely peel her wet clothes off. Every movement was awkward and painful, but the warm water felt like heaven against her frozen body. She avoided washing her bruise, afraid to touch it.

She patted dry with a towel and double-checked the locks on the doors and windows, making sure the curtains covered every square inch. With all the lights on, she slipped under the covers in her towel. She didn't feel comfortable naked, even though a towel barely counted as clothing. She felt exposed.

Even though she knew she was far away, she couldn't shake the feeling that Nick would find her. He hunted down criminals as a police officer. To think he couldn't track down his own wife would be dangerous.

Each time her eyes finally slid closed, some noise would shake her out of sleep. Her mind kept playing the "what if" game. What if he found her? What if she had to keep running? What if she never found her freedom again?

As she stared up at the ceiling, she focused on the sounds of the waves outside. The man named Jack drifted into her thoughts. Charismatic, for sure. She could still taste the lobster drenched in butter. That meal must've cost a fortune. She felt bad that she'd slipped out of the restaurant without saying goodbye, but he had been in the crowd, and she didn't want to attract more attention by showcasing her bruised face. The note she left thanked him with a tip. Even though he refused to let her pay for the meal, when she got on her feet again, she'd pay him back for his generosity. She'd walk back into the restaurant, clean and dry, and hand him the money. He'd smile that pearly white smile and show off those eyes that looked like a shallow tide over a summer afternoon sea. She'd show him she wasn't that beaten girl who needed his sympathy, but a woman taking her life back.

It just didn't feel that way yet.

The faint rhythm of the ocean lapping against the shore whispered in the room, and she noticed the rain had stopped. She rolled over and forced her eyes shut. Her mind focused on each wave, visualizing the shoreline. She imagined digging her bare feet in the sand, sitting on a granite boulder, and watching the horizon. Before Rachael had a chance to imagine seagulls floating above her, she had fallen into a deep sleep.

But it didn't last long. She woke, jolting up in bed. Her heart raced as her eyes darted around the lit-up hotel room. Her head jerked around as she checked her surroundings. She had forgotten for just a split second where she was, but then she remembered she was in Camden Cove.

She fell back into the bed, but after tossing and turning, Rachael got up. It wasn't even half past three and still too early to start the day, but Rachael was done with sleeping.

With the hotel Wi-Fi, she looked up the local news in Providence. No police reports of a missing woman. No pictures of Rachael's face posted in the corner of the screen. She wondered if he had already begun looking for her, or if he'd lay low. He wouldn't want to draw attention. He was smart enough to know her beaten face would only bring trouble at this point.

She wondered what *his* face looked like.

The local news had nothing other than a couple of burglaries.

She'd been gone for over twenty-four hours. If someone wanted to know where she was, it didn't make the news.

Rachael collected some damp clothes from where they hung and pulled the hairdryer out from the wall, drying them enough for the day. She avoided the bathroom mirror for as long as she could, but finally set the dryer down and leaned against the counter. Gently, with the tips of her fingers, she examined her cheek. The bruise had darkened into a deep shade of purple, the blood pooled along her jawline and up along her ear. She slowly opened and closed her jaw. It felt more tender than yesterday, but she was lucky it wasn't broken. She winced as she touched around her eye. No makeup would cover that.

How was she going to find a job with a face like hers?

Grabbing a plastic cup from the counter, she took a drink of water, her hand shaking. She went back to drying her clothes, the fabric blowing across her hand. For now, she had to focus on finding work. There had to be a place that needed an extra waitress, or a housekeeper. Hopefully she could find a rental for the winter. Someone had to have something. She had enough money to survive for a bit.

With as much matte foundation she could layer on, her eye seemed a bit more presentable, but she wasn't sure if the bad makeup job would attract more attention than the black eye. She decided to put effort into her hair, parting it to cover up the side of her face as much as possible. With her clothes decently dried, she grabbed her bag, wrapped her wallet around her waist, then headed to the continental breakfast in the lobby.

Behind the counter stood an elderly man in a red turtleneck with a pair of glasses sitting on the end of his nose, his attention was on his phone when Rachael walked into the small room.

"Morning," he said, but not bothering to look up as Rachael reached the long table set up in the corner. A quite impressive arrangement had been set out. All types of pastries, jellies in glass jars, fresh fruit, along with whipped butter over ice.

The man set his phone down. "If you need anything, let me know."

Rachael nodded.

"Today's going to be a beautiful one," the man carried on, his tone chipper. "And we deserve it, with all that rain."

Then he looked out over the counter at Rachael. Did he make a face?

"Oh, dear, oh my." He leaned forward in his chair from behind the counter and studied Rachael. "That's quite a bruise."

The comment made Rachael wince, but she tried to cover it up. "The end table won the fight. Fell on it when I got out of bed in the middle of the night, a couple days ago."

The man nodded as though the same kind of thing had happened to him. "Geez, it sure did win."

He continued to stare, not realizing his overstep, even when Rachael moved away from him and toward the food.

"You can take whatever you like." He stood up, leaving his station and walking into the dining room behind Rachael, grabbed a cup and filled it with coffee. "Are you on vacation?"

Rachael took a plate and grabbed a croissant. "Sort of."

"Make sure you hit the bakery down the road," he suggested. "It's where we get all our pastries, but they're so much better fresh. Greatest chocolate croissants you'll ever eat. The chocolate melts in your mouth."

Rachael didn't look up from the mini donuts. "I'll be sure to check it out."

"And if you are looking for some lobster, The Fish Market is your best bet."

Wasn't that the restaurant she was at, last night? She almost asked, but the man dumped cream into his coffee.

"I'm Henry. I'm here most mornings." He offered his hand, and Rachael slowly offered her own.

"Rachael."

Henry stood there and sipped his coffee. They stood in silence at first, but then Henry started up the conversation again. "It's a shame most of the stores are closed this time of year, but you can find some nice places still open. The Country Store always has some cute souvenirs. You'll definitely have the beach to yourself, if you don't mind blowing around a bit."

"I'd prefer to be alone." Rachael slowly made her way down the table, grabbed a few more pastries. She headed toward the small kiosk for a map of the area that had dozens of brochures of local attractions. Some place must need someone to do something.

Henry watched as Rachael walked toward the door. "You have a great day now."

"You, too." Rachael pointed to the stack of newspapers by the door. "Do you mind if I take one?"

Henry waved a hand. "Absolutely not."

Rachael grabbed one and headed out to the parking lot. She walked down Main Street to Harbor Lane, and that's when she saw it.

The ocean.

Right before her eyes, the rising sun glistened off the water, hanging low along the horizon. She stood frozen, watching as waves rolled onto the granite shoreline. Tears sprung to her eyes as she saw a seagull gliding above the water, floating in the wind. She once thought she'd never feel any kind of freedom again, but as she watched the sun rise in the east, she felt as free as the bird.

Off in the distance, a bell rang out a slow count. The draw-bridge in the harbor rose as a lobster boat passed beneath. Its red hull parted the water, coasting along on its way out to sea, sounding its horn.

As though she were spellbound, Rachael walked toward the water, passing the diner and the Country Store. She walked past a bakery, a candy shop, and some gift boutiques with *Closed for the Season* signs in the windows. She quickened her pace down Harbor Lane, remembering some of the buildings from the night before. As she reached the end of the road, she stood facing the water, standing along the edge of the Atlantic Ocean.

She looked out over the harbor to the granite bluffs, then back down the road noticing another sign, *The Fish* Market. In the dark, and with the rain coming down so hard, she hadn't noticed that the restaurant hung on the edge of the sea.

She wondered if the man she met last night was the owner. Pretty young, to own a waterfront restaurant. It easily had the best view in the whole town. What was the saying? Location, location, location?

Glimmers of light reflected off the water, beckoning her, and she didn't notice when the door to the restaurant opened until Jack stepped out. A wave of warmth flushed her body as he immediately smiled.

He lifted his hand to shield the sun from his eyes. "Rachael, right?"

He wore a white chef's coat with a pair of grey pants that fit him perfectly. His gaze went straight to her. "You headed to the beach?"

"I didn't get to see much of it last night."

"If you haven't checked it out, there's a path along the coast." He pointed beyond the restaurant to a gravel trail winding down along the granite boulders. She stayed quiet, not sure what there was to say, but he seemed comfortable to fill in for her. One of those guys that hadn't been touched by the weight of the world. "It goes down a mile or so, but it's well worth your time. No better views."

"Except from your restaurant." She pointed to the shingled building.

A look of pride filled his face. "It's my family's business."

"Thanks again for last night." She instinctively wrapped her arms around her wallet. "I can pay you back."

He shook his head, rolling back on the balls of his feet. "That won't be necessary, even your tip wasn't necessary. It's how we welcome newcomers to Camden Cove."

"By feeding them surf and turf?" She doubted that.

"Only if you're kicked out, first." He was clearly trying to lighten the mood. "Are you staying in Camden Cove long?"

She shook her head. With his boyish charm, no doubt other women got lost in his intoxicating gaze, but not her. Not any longer. "I should get going. Thanks again for letting me escape the weather last night."

She rushed away and headed back toward Main Street. She had to find some sort of work. Waiting tables, hosting, washing dishes — anything. She needed money to get moving on, because if everyone in this town ended up being as nosy as that guy, she'd never be able to hide here.

She hit the Country Store first, standing in line, pretending to look at the candy shelf next to the check out.

"Did you find everything okay?" a woman asked behind the register.

"Yes, thanks. I wondered if you were looking for any help?" Rachael asked.

The woman's happy demeanor showed pity as she shook her head. "Honestly? I think you're going to have a hard time finding something this time of year."

Rachael's hopes fell to the floor.

"Can I help you find anything else?"

Rachael flew out of the store as fast as her emotions came over her. What was she going to do?

The rest of her day went the same. Most places were closed for the season. The diner took her information, but wished her good luck. Like a compass directing her north, by mid-afternoon, she stood in front of the tavern. It looked the same as it had all those years ago.

She opened the door and stepped inside, her eyes adjusting to the darkness inside. It took a second to realize she was the only one in the whole place.

"Hello?" she called out, looking around. There were about a dozen tables in the middle of the room. In the corner, a wood stove sat dark. The place looked like the inside of a ship, with brass portholes hanging on the walls.

She recognized him as soon as he walked out from the back. He appeared surprised to see someone standing there. He had aged quite a bit since the last time she had seen him, but there was no mistaking him.

"What can I do for you?" he asked.

"Are you open?" She didn't know where to start.

"Did the sign say otherwise?" He sounded a bit irritated by her question.

"I guess not."

"Can I get you something?"

She could see the resemblance in his eyes. The dark stone color. "I would love a drink."

He looked at the clock, then back at her, and shrugged. She wasn't sure if he noticed her eye or not, but she could tell he was trying to figure her out. "Well?"

"Well, what?"

"What do you want to drink?"

"Oh, right." She didn't really want a drink, but she *was* in a tavern. Would it seem strange to order water? "I'll have a Coke."

"One Coke, coming up." He picked up a glass and shoved it into a sink of ice. "You from around here?"

She shook her head. "Nope."

"Huh, you look familiar." He filled her glass and slid it across to her. "You been here before, then?"

She almost came out with it right then, but took a sip of the soda instead, chickening out. "My grandfather lives around here."

"That's probably it." The old man grabbed a towel and wiped down the counter next to her. "Who's your grandfather, then?"

She pushed her glass aside and looked up. She took a deep breath, then said, "Finnegan McCabe."

He stopped wiping and looked up at her. He didn't say anything.

"Hi Pops, it's me, Rachael." She sat up straighter. "I came up to visit."

"I see that." He crossed his arms, his body rigid. "I have a feeling you're here for more than just a visit."

She swallowed. "It's been a long time."

"A really long time." He glanced at her bruise. "I haven't spoken to you or your mother since you last were here."

She nodded, not knowing what to say. It had been more than twenty years. As a little girl, the time they lived with Finn was magical. He brought her to the beach, got her candy and ice cream at night, everything was perfect until her dad came back. He took her mom and her that night back to Rhode Island. Rachael cried the whole way back, and her parents never talked about it.

"I'm no charity center, so if you're looking for a handout, then you should just keep looking." His voice was gruffer than before. "You'd be better off finding that loser father of yours."

His words stung. "I was just swinging through town, that's all." She stood up from her stool, placing a five on the bar. "Thanks for the drink."

When she walked toward the door, she heard him say, "How long are you in town?"

She stopped and turned toward him, shrugging. "I'm not sure yet."

He nodded, as though he understood. "Well, why don't you take a seat and I'll get you something to eat."

Jack thought about Rachael taking off down the road, leaving him in the dust, or really the morning sun. She walked with purpose. The most intriguing woman he'd ever met and she practically ran away from him for the second time in less than twelve hours. Definitely a new low for him.

He hadn't stopped thinking about her since she stepped inside the restaurant the previous night, dripping from head to toe.

What was she doing all alone in Camden Cove at this time of year? Did that bruise have anything to do with it?

Just as well. He didn't have time to get involved with anyone right now. Not with all the work he wanted to do on the restaurant. Not to mention, he'd already dealt with enough needy women in his lifetime. He hardly needed another one.

As the day wore on, though, his mind kept returning to Rachael who showed up at his door. Well, the restaurant's door, but close enough. And what was her deal today? He had been nothing but kind and generous to her.

It was what he was thinking in the market when he ran into his realtor, Colleen Connolly, who seemed pleased to see him. That was what usually happened with women. He drew them in, not repelled them.

"Well, well, well, Jack Williams, it's been too long." She leaned against the carriage's handle, her cleavage deepening as her arms squeezed her chest. "I didn't know you had a dog."

"Good afternoon, Colleen." He smiled back, looking at the can of dog food in his hands. "I don't."

One eyebrow lifted as she tilted her head to the side.

"There's a stray down by the beach." He threw the can into his basket. "I caught it eating out of my dumpsters."

"Jack Williams, you are a gentleman." She leaned harder on her cart. "If you're not busy, you should come by, and we could talk about your rental property."

He smiled as she winked after her offer, but shook his head. "I have to get back to the restaurant."

"You work too hard." She pushed her cart a bit closer to him. "So, I heard you met the new girl in town."

He suspected she was referring to Rachael. It figured the whole town would be talking about the beautiful stranger, this time of year. He nodded. "I have."

"Christine Winters told me she crashed your sister's wedding last night." He had a feeling Colleen was bringing this up because she hadn't been included in the celebration.

"She came to eat at the restaurant, she didn't know it was closed for an event." he said simply. Something bothered him by the way she fished for information about Rachael.

"I heard she's looking to stay around," she continued. "She was asking for work all over town."

"What?" This surprised him. She was looking to stay? "Where?"

"I saw her talking to Louis over at the diner this morning, then I heard she was in here, earlier." Colleen clicked her tongue a few times. "That black eye says she'll bring nothing but trouble, if you ask me."

A sudden surge of protectiveness came over him. "She's not trouble."

She waved at him, dismissing it. "Well, I should probably head out to my next showing. See you later, gorgeous."

She pushed around him and down the aisle.

Jack was left standing, trying to register what it meant that Rachael was looking for work. Her accent certainly wasn't local, more like Boston or Rhode Island. And at this time of year? Nobody came up at this time of year. Unless they were trying to get away from something.

Or someone.

He shook his head. She could've fallen or gotten into an accident. Why did he suspect something terrible had happened to her?

Because of the way she flinched when he grabbed her, as she slipped in the restaurant. The fear in her eyes as he helped her to her feet. Whatever made her come up here, he hoped would never find her.

He picked up the rest of his items and got out of there. For the rest of the day, his mind continued to spin about Rachael, and soon he stood in the same spot outside the restaurant, remembering his encounter with her that morning as he locked up. He set off, walking up the street to meet his brother at Finn's. After the past few days, with his sister's wedding, sitting back with a good, stiff drink sounded perfect.

He pulled up the collar of his jacket as he walked up Harbor Lane. The autumn night sky had swallowed up any warmth from the day. Smoke from a nearby wood stove wafted in the air. Winter would soon be approaching. The crunching of leaves under his feet proved it. The winter season brought a solace to the town of Camden Cove. The tourists stayed away. Residents took refuge indoors and slowed down. Those who lived off the water welcomed the forced respite. People were grateful for another successful season, and taking time to prepare for the new one yet to come.

He rubbed his hands together as he stepped inside, looking around for his brother. As soon as he caught sight of the bar, he noticed Rachael standing behind the counter with the owner, Finn. She set two glasses on an already full tray of a dozen or more drinks. She grabbed the tray and balanced it on her hand like a seasoned server as she walked out from behind the bar. She placed the drinks on a table on the other side of the room, then turned to the next table, where Matt was sitting. Jack practically pushed Bill Garneau over, trying to get there.

"What can I get for you tonight?" he heard her ask.

Matt waved as soon as he saw Jack approaching. "I'll take two boilermakers." He nodded at Jack. "One for me and one for my brother, here."

She turned around and her mouth immediately dropped open.

"Hey, Rachael. Twice in one day." He caught his breath from his dash across the tavern. "You working here?"

"Hey." Her eyes widened as she stood frozen, a look of actual pain on her face. She then ignored him, returning her attention to Matt. "Two boilermakers, coming up."

Matt watched him as she raced away for the bar. "You really have a way with women."

Jack peeked behind him, pulling the stool underneath him as

he sat down. "She's the woman who came in from the rain last night."

Matt took another look, and Jack followed his gaze. Dang, she was good-looking, especially as she poured the shots of his favorite whiskey. Her hair was different, falling along her shoulders in soft waves. She didn't dress fancy, just in a t-shirt and jeans which accented her curves more than he wished to admit.

Heaven help him.

"Looks like you might be a bit smitten."

"She's gorgeous." Jack wouldn't deny it. Nothing wrong with being attracted to a beautiful woman. Yet, something told him that the way the electric current ran through his body every time he looked at her, meant he was more than just smitten.

"She doesn't seem your type."

"What's my type?" Jack pushed off his elbows and sat up, slightly defensive. First Colleen Connolly and now Matt, what was getting into him?

"Well, she obviously comes with a bit of baggage, wouldn't you say?"

"Where's your wife, again?" Jack didn't mean to be a jerk, but his younger brother didn't get it.

"Don't change the subject," Matt said. "Just 'cause you have the hots—"

"Didn't Justine want you home early, tonight?" Jack laid on the sarcasm, but smiled as Rachael returned to the table.

"Actually, she's out with her friends."

Rachael set their drinks on the table, making no eye contact. The electric current raced through to his toes, even though she avoided him.

"Can I get you anything else?" She directed the question to Matt, her eyes skipping over Jack, making the current rev up even more.

"I heard you might be staying in town." Jack avoided his brother's eyes. "We're always looking for some more help at the restaurant."

"No. Thanks."

Just as he opened his mouth to try to make her reconsider she walked away, taking his ego with her and leaving a sweet smell of jasmine… or was it rose? Jack leaned back, catching his breath. Was it hot in there?

Matt shook his head as he quietly laughed to himself. He raised his eyebrows. "I don't think she likes you."

Jack shrugged as he pulled at his collar, letting in some air. With his other hand, he held up his shot glass toward his brother. "She'll like me."

Matt tapped his glass against Jack's. "I think you've got this one wrong."

Jack let out a huff. "I'm not usually the one who's chasing."

Matt held his shot of whiskey above his beer. "A hundred says she won't give you the time of day."

"Double that, and I'll have her chasing after me." Jack dropped his shot of whiskey.

Matt laughed as they drank the beer down. "You might as well pay me now."

Jack made a face, but he couldn't keep his eyes off Rachael as she poured more drinks.

"Look who's decided to drag themselves out from the bowels of humanity." Matt groaned behind his beer as Freddy Harrington and his cronies stepped inside Finn's. "The biggest donkey of them all."

Freddy sat on the other side of the tavern, far enough that their view was obscured by the rest of the patrons, but close enough that Freddy's irritating voice could be heard over the crowd.

Jack kept his eye on Rachael as she walked up to Freddy. He instantly did his thing, leaning close and showing off in front of her. Even from across the room, he could hear the obnoxious laugh. He had probably already told her who his father was by now.

"I haven't seen you here before." Freddy's voice carried across the room. He played with his expensive watch for her to see. "You must be new."

Jack leaned to the side to get a better view, but he could only see Rachael from behind. He couldn't hear what she had said back, but Freddy kept his donkey smile on his face. From below, Jack noticed Freddy's hand suddenly reach over toward Rachael, but someone walked by, blocking his view, and he couldn't see where it ended up. Did Freddy just grab her?

With the way Freddy smirked, Jack slid off his chair to see if Rachael was okay, but when she turned around, her expression appeared the same as before. He must not have seen what he thought.

"Did you see that?" Jack pointed at Freddy as Matt gave him a face.

"What's with you? Freddy's always a jerk."

Bad blood had always run between the two families, even before his sister Lauren started dating the youngest of the three Harrington brothers. Jack cringed at the thought of his sweet baby sister with a Harrington.

His focus stayed on Rachael even after she left Freddy's table. Behind the bar, she didn't look frazzled or even the slightest bit uncomfortable. No doubt she had been a waitress before. A good waitress, too. She carried the full tray to Freddy and his friends with ease. Her wrist didn't quiver under its weight. No drink even wavered. She leaned over, handing each of the men their order. When she reached Freddy, her wrist suddenly bent and the tray wobbled to the right, spilling the glass and sending the full drink into Freddy's crotch before she grabbed the glass.

"What the—" Freddy jumped up out of his chair, wiping the liquid off his pants, but it was too late. His whole lap was soaked.

Rachael tucked the tray under her arm. "Let me know if I can get you anything else."

"What kind of waitress are you?!" Freddy grabbed a handful of napkins. His friends all laughed as he scrubbed the wetness off his pants.

She wiped away the splatter from the beer off the table's surface. "Enjoy."

Without looking back, she walked away as Freddy had a meltdown in the middle of the tavern.

"Looks like he *did* do something," Matt whispered, laughing.

"She purposely spilled that drink on me!" Freddy pushed back his chair. He pounded toward the bar as Rachael set the tray on the counter, stepping behind it and staring Freddy down. She looked like a jaguar about to pounce.

Before Jack could change his mind, he jumped out of his chair and moved in front of Freddy.

"What are you doing, Williams?" Freddy pushed his hands against Jack's chest, but he didn't budge.

"Why don't you cool down?" Jack pushed Freddy back. He stumbled backwards a bit.

Freddy scowled. "Finn, you going to do something about your new waitress?"

"Maybe keep your hands where they belong, and you wouldn't have to worry about the service." Jack purposely spoke loud enough that others could hear.

"Really, Williams?" Freddy puffed out his chest. Jack smirked at the confidence Freddy exuded, especially with Matt suddenly standing behind him. Both Williamses easily stood four inches taller than Freddy.

Rachael untied the apron's strings and pulled it over her head. She walked over to Finn and handed it to him. "I dropped the drink in his lap."

"That won't be necessary, Rachael." Finn pushed back her apron and crossed his arms. "Freddy, you can take your business somewhere else."

Jack smirked as Freddy's face fell in shock. He pulled out his wallet and threw twenties on the bar. "Don't worry about the tab."

Freddy huffed and put his hands on his hips. "Are you kidding me? Do you know what kind of business I bring in here?"

Finn folded his arms across his chest. Thirty years his senior, he could probably still take a pretty boy like Freddy. "Not the kind of business I want."

Jack smiled at Finn. He probably would take a hit, but the old man did the right thing. Jack watched as Freddy slithered back to his friends, glowering.

"You'll be hearing about this." Freddy's threat was empty. He grabbed his coat and pounded the door open.

As soon as Freddy and his friends left, the volume picked up and people went back to their own conversations. Jack spun around, half expecting Rachael to be next to him, swooning. The two hundred dollars practically in his hands. Instead, Rachael stared him down like a bull ready to charge.

"What did you think you were doing?"

Guess not. He looked back at the door, then back at her, confused by her reaction. "Um, you're welcome."

She let out a huff and crossed her arms across her chest. Her weight shifted as her hip swayed lower. "Wow."

"You don't know what he was going to do." He wouldn't want his sisters having to deal with such a slime ball.

Her eyes narrowed at him. "I don't need rescuing."

"What's wrong with a little help?" He looked over to Matt, whose smile grew. Was she seriously upset with him?

"I didn't need your help. He wasn't going to do anything." She picked up the tray.

"Look, my mom raised me to be a gentleman." He caught her eyes and tried to hold on, trying to gauge what the anger was all about. Even though the voice inside his head told him not to ask, the words fell out of his mouth. "Did someone do that to you?"

Her hand immediately covered the side of her face. Her jaw clenched. She turned and charged away.

What had made him ask her that?

He walked back to the table, where Matt was now sitting with two new beers. Matt slid one over to Jack. "This is going to be the easiest two hundred dollars I've ever made."

Rachael wiped down the tables, then put the chairs up on top. After a good sweep, she took off her apron and walked behind the counter.

"Nice job, tonight." Finn stood behind the cash register, closing out the till. He flipped up the plastic handles that held down the cash.

"Sorry about that guy." She patted the wallet strapped to her belly, now full of tips. She did feel bad, hoping she didn't hurt his business. Finn shook his head.

He slammed the register drawer shut. "He's an imbecile, so I'm not real worried about it."

She smiled, but she could tell by the look on his face that he wasn't so sure about her. He acted like he didn't want to be bothered by her, but insisted she cover the night shift when she mentioned she was looking for work. She tried to refuse, but he didn't let her say no. She wondered if he regretted letting her work there. He definitely lost a steady customer on account of her behavior.

"I wish I had more to offer you in terms of work." He sounded like a business owner, not a grandfather. "But I don't really need help during the winter months." His words made her heart sink. "But you're good. I'm sure you'll find something."

She nodded, reaching out her hand toward his. "Thanks, I mean it."

"Around here, The Fish Market is probably your best bet." His hand was rough and calloused. "I could call the owner, Jack."

She shook her head and stepped away. "I'll be okay."

He nodded, but she could tell he didn't believe her. "You got a place to stay?"

"I'm staying at the inn down the road," she said, though she doubted she'd stick around much past Thursday. She'd scoot farther up the coast. Maybe even go to Canada. "Let me know if you need more help."

"Your mom know you're here?" he asked.

She shook her head.

He nodded. "Come by tomorrow, and you can take the night shift again."

"What?" He wanted her to work now? "Are you sure?"

"Do you think I'd ask if I was unsure?"

She smiled, because she remembered his gruffness from when she was a kid. She walked toward him to thank him, but he walked away from her, through the door to the kitchen.

"Thanks," she said, to the door slapping closed.

Once outside, the wind whipped her hair against her face and she wished she had more than a sweatshirt. In the background, the repetition of waves smashing onto the shore created a calming rhythm, but her nerves were still on edge. Images of that man rushing at her, his eyes lost in irrational anger, flooded her mind. Then, images of Nick rushing at her. How different his eyes had been, like those of an animal.

When she got inside her hotel room, she poured all the complimentary salts and soaps into the water, then soaked in the tub. Baths had been her only solitude before she left. She'd bathe for hours, soaking. She didn't care when the water got cold. It was the only time she could lock the door and dream of escaping.

After she dried off, she lay on the bed for a while and thought of Nick back in the early days, when she first met him. How nice he had been to her. He'd send her flowers at work, and everyone would tell her how lucky she was. He'd take her out to fancy restaurants and let her order anything she wanted. They'd talk for hours. They'd laugh a lot. He felt so safe in the beginning.

She picked up her phone and opened up the browser. She wanted to check the news but stopped herself. Instead, she searched restaurants in Camden Cove. The Fish Market popped up at the top of the screen. As the Wi-Fi loaded, she thought about Jack jumping to her defense. He didn't even hesitate to stand up for her with that creep. Was he being kind? Or was he being kind of crazy? Five stars popped up as soon as a review site opened. Comment after comment about the excellence of the food. Everyone raved and credited the young executive chef.

It figured, he was perfect.

She threw her phone on the other side of the bed, her arm a bit sore from holding trays of drinks all night. The work had been hard, but she liked it. She missed working. The only reason she had quit her waitressing job was because Nick had encouraged her to go to school full time. A dream come true.

In the beginning, things had been good, really good. By the time she realized how tight his grip was on her, it had been too late. Before she knew it, he'd made her check in when she got to class, and tell him when she was leaving. Then, after a year of school, he decided to stop paying for classes, convincing her she didn't need to work. She didn't know just when it started, but soon she lived like a prisoner in their home.

She couldn't even go to her mother's house without being interrogated. Her mother had been sympathetic to her situation, but never enough to encourage her to leave. She had lost touch with most of her friends, since they still worked and went to school. There were a couple of girls she stayed in touch with, but she never really told them the truth. She was too ashamed.

Nick had been right to worry. The little freedom he did give her, she used to plan her escape. Every time she left the house, she'd take an extra sweater or other item, and hide it at her mother's place. For almost a year, she'd squirreled away money and other essentials. A full year of planning, preparing, and praying he wouldn't find out.

Today had been the first time in a long time she felt in complete control of her life. Until Jack decided to step in.

What he'd done had been nice. He had been nothing *but* nice.

But so had Nick.

And she'd promised herself that she'd never let another person control her again.

Ever.

No matter how nice he was.

34

CHAPTER 3

$\mathcal{T}$he sound of church bells woke Rachael up. Her eyes popped open in instant panic. Where was he?

Her eyes darted around the room. Then a wave of relief washed over her. Nick wasn't there. She was alone.

Even with the lights on and the shades closed, sunlight filtered through the sides of the windows. Had she slept past sunrise? And for a solid five hours? She hadn't slept that late in years.

Laying back in bed, she grabbed the pillows and cozied into them. She could go back to sleep. She didn't need to get up, she had nowhere to go, no one to listen to. Then a horn sounded. A horn from a boat.

She flung the covers off and drew back the shades, blinking in the sun. The clear, blue sky met the edge of the water, and the two almost blended together.

She wanted to go to the ocean.

At Henry's insistence, she took more than her share of food from the continental breakfast, said goodbye, and took off down Main Street to Harbor Lane. All the shops were closed, except a bakery and the Country Store. When she walked by The Fish

Market, her stomach did a little belly flop, surprising her. What was that about?

She hurried her steps, but slanted her eyes to make it seem as though she wasn't looking at the restaurant. Not that she wanted to see Jack. She didn't want to see him. She wanted to walk the path he had mentioned. That was all. She wanted to sit on the beach and watch the boats float out to sea as the seagulls flew above.

She almost started to jog, hurrying past Jack's restaurant to reach the mouth of the trail. A gravel path ran parallel to the Atlantic Ocean. She stopped and took in a deep breath. Her hair blew against her face as she exhaled, every cell in her body tingling as she took in another breath. The tangy, salty air filled her lungs. A call from a seagull soaring above the water made her look up. Her eyes burned and watered as she watched the seagull swoop low to the water's surface, then glide back up into the blue sky.

How did she get here? All alone, broken and ashamed? What Finn must think of her. She closed her eyes and a tear escaped down her cheek.

The seagull cried out, sounding as though it flew right above her head. She looked up as it swayed in the wind above the water. She didn't want to be a victim any longer. If Nick hadn't come by now, maybe he wasn't going to. Maybe she had freedom, for real. With her hand covering the sun, she watched the seagull, wishing she could fly even further away where no one could find her.

Jack pulled open the can's cover and dumped the wet mush into a plastic container. He filled a bag of dry food and stuffed it into his pocket. The last time he saw the stray, it was digging in his trash. He had scared the dog, and it took off down the coastal trail. Hopefully, it found some sort of shelter or empty shed. The nights were getting colder. Maine's brutal winter was fast approaching.

His sister Elizabeth, the local vet, thought it was likely a stray. More likely than not, it had been abandoned, since there were no missing dogs that fit the description. The black dog had a white patch like a butterfly on its chest. The mark made it easily identifiable, and the visibility of the dog's protruding bones made him think that if it was missing, it was a long way from home.

Somebody needed to help him.

He opened his sliding glass door and stepped onto his deck. The Atlantic was only a couple hundred yards from his doorstep. His house sat on the cliffs just off the Coastal Trail, one of the only cottages that had been winterized. It took him almost a year to complete, since the whole place had to be gutted and rebuilt, but it was worth it every time he stepped out onto his deck and saw the view.

He replaced the empty container on the back deck with fresh food, and decided to take a walk down the trail before his run.

The day was perfect. A blue sky. A slight breeze. One of the last few days before that breeze turned into the bone-chilling winter wind. Off in the distance, a lobster boat hauled up some traps. His brother had probably been out on the water for hours.

He had almost given up, when he caught sight of the black dog down on the beach in the alcove. But it wasn't alone. Rachael held out her hand, palm up. The dog leaned its head closer, sitting on its haunches as Rachael sat on a rock. With Jack, the dog wouldn't even go near him, let alone sit down next to him. He watched for a second, then slowly took a step, but his foot slipped on a patch of sandy pebbles. The dog flinched, looking in his direction. Rachael swung around and scowled as the dog jumped away from her. The glare she gave him made him freeze. He held out his hands in a silent gesture of apology.

Fumbling in his pocket, he grabbed the baggie of kibble and held it out, as though it explained his presence, but her eyes still sent out a smoldering anger that made her look even hotter.

The dog scampered back onto the beach, watching Jack. Rachael held out the piece of food again. Was that a donut? Jack stood frozen as the dog timidly stepped up to Rachael, snatched the food out of her hand, then took off running up the cove.

She watched the dog until it was out of sight, then swung around, hands fisted on her hips. "What do you think you're doing?"

He climbed down the rocks into the inlet. "I'm sorry." He held out the baggie to her. "I was actually looking for that dog. I think he's a stray."

Her eyes darted back and forth between him and the bag of food. Then she narrowed them. "You just happened to come looking for the dog?"

"Yes."

Her eyes narrowed even more.

"Why else would I have dog food when I don't even own a dog?" He shook the bag again. He understood she wanted to be cautious around strangers. However, he had been nothing but kind to this woman. He opened his door and fed her. Stood up for her. She may not have wanted him to get involved with Freddy Harrington, but shoot him for wanting to help her out. That had to say something about his character, but her eyes only grew cooler.

Then, her fists loosened and her arms dropped to her sides. "Next time, let someone know you're there, instead of sneaking up on them."

She sat back down on the rock, looking out at the water. He stood far enough away to give her space.

"I'm sorry about last night." He stuffed his hands into his pockets. "It's just that I know that guy, and he's a —"

"A jerk?" she finished for him.

He chuckled, nervous. "Yeah, you can say that."

She pulled her legs up onto the rock, wrapping her arms around her knees and resting her chin on top. "Thanks."

He smiled, surprised. "You're welcome. So, you're working at the Tavern?"

"Surprisingly, Finn didn't fire me."

"He's a pretty good guy." Was this a truce? Did she finally figure out *he* might be a good guy?

"Yeah, he is." She nodded her head.

Working at Finn's, she'd earn petty cash, definitely not enough to live on. Not like his servers earned at The Fish Market. Finn's never lacked for customers, but they were locals, fishermen and their wives, whose money was tight. They didn't leave the kind of tips the patrons at his restaurant did.

"I could actually use extra help at the restaurant." He was glad Matt wasn't there, because he definitely didn't need help. He had officially lost his mind. He stood there waiting for a reaction. "The offer still stands, if you're looking for work."

"I'm good." She kept her gaze on the water. "Finn gave me a couple more shifts."

This surprised him. Finn had his staff for years, and most of the time it was just him. Now, not only did this woman stroll into town two days ago, she already had a job. The rational, business side of him couldn't let it go. "You'd make double what you make working all weekend at Finn's."

Her coolness switched to fire before he finished his sentence. "Thanks, but I'm good."

She got up off the rock, picked up her bag and wiped off the sand from its bottom, ready to take off.

"You wouldn't have to work as much."

"I don't need the job." She swung her bag on her shoulder, stepping across the rocky beach toward the trail.

He chuckled. "You're more stubborn than my sisters, and I thought they were impossible to beat."

She faced him. "I'm not stubborn. I just don't need to be pushed around."

"Is that what you think I'm doing?"

She stopped and threw a look at him. "I don't need your help. I don't need anyone's help."

~

Rachael tightened the straps of her bag as she walked up the trail from the cove.

"Where are you staying?" Jack yelled after her. His voice almost drowned out by the waves.

For some reason, she stopped and faced him, not answering and watched as he sat down on a rock, making himself comfortable. He gave off a feeling of calm that flittered her nerves even more. He didn't seem to notice her mood, or didn't care. And as much as she wanted this conversation over, she couldn't make herself move from where she stood.

His eyebrows furrowed. "Is there any place still open?"

She let out a loud sigh. "Not for long."

It looked as though he stopped himself from saying something. His mouth froze opened, but no words came out.

"Yes?"

"Listen, I know you don't want to take my help, for whatever reason."

"You're right, I don't."

"But I honestly have a one-room apartment that needs to be filled." He took his finger and made an X over his heart. "I swear to you."

He just happened to have an empty apartment? She wasn't even going to give him an answer. She shifted her bag's strap and walked away.

"It's above the restaurant." He stood up, following behind her up the trail. "It's small, a studio with a bathroom and a shower, but the best view in all of Camden Cove."

The view from the restaurant flashed in her head. A dream spot, for sure. Something she definitely couldn't afford. "No, thanks."

"You already have a place to stay?"

She didn't say anything. She was suddenly irritated that he'd called her bluff. She had imagined that Finn would embrace her when she confessed who she was, like he did when she was a kid. He'd offer his help, and a place to stay. She remembered his house in town.

"So you don't need a place to stay…?" he trailed off. He flung his hand out. "Why won't you accept my help?"

"Why won't you leave anything alone?" she snapped back.

They both huffed.

"Good luck finding something at this time of year." He walked in front of her up the trail.

She sped up and past him. "Don't worry, I'm not sticking around." Who did this guy think he was?

"You're not?"

She had already said too much. "Look, just leave me alone."

"Fine." He stopped, falling behind her. "Good luck, Rachael."

As he climbed down the rocks, reality hit her. Where *was* she going to go, after this? She had no car, she had just enough money for first and last months' rent, but not much more if she wanted to eat. What if she couldn't find another place at this time of the year? What if she ended up without any money?

"Wait!"

He had reached the head of another trail. Her head dropped as she gave in. He didn't turn around. He waited for what she had to say.

Begrudgingly, she asked, "How much is the apartment?"

He turned with that smile on his face. Her belly did another flip-flop. She wanted to hate him, but there was something about him. Something made her want to stay where she was.

"What can you afford?"

Her face flushed, and the way he looked at her bothered her more, because he knew she did need help. She hated that he called her out.

Then, before she could answer, he said, "I can take you to see it, if you want?"

"Okay."

"Will you be okay climbing back up to the trail?" he asked, pointing to the footpath that climbed up the cliff.

She grabbed her bag and climbed the rocks with no trouble at all. She might be giving in about the apartment, but she could still climb up some rocks on her own. She heard him laughing behind her, but focused on the seagulls flying above.

"That's the way to the apartment." He pointed to the left and let her take the lead, walking behind her along the winding path. "That's my place over there."

A small cottage sat back from the rocky cliff. She noticed the proximity to the water and to the restaurant. He couldn't have found a better spot.

"That's quite a commute." The two-story cottage had faded gray shingles and white trim. Windows covered the whole back end, facing out toward the water. Either Jack had a very successful restaurant, or he had an incredible bank account, or both. Either way, she couldn't help but hope that someday, she'd just have a place to call home.

"I had been waiting for years for one of these cottages to sell, while I lived above the restaurant. I just moved in at the beginning of summer. Then some college kids rented it out."

"The rent must be steep for an apartment on the ocean?" The view alone probably cost more than her entire life savings.

"Not really." He grimaced. "Not too many people want to stay in Camden Cove during the winter."

As they reached the end of the trail, she noticed more cars in the parking lot. The sun had warmed up the day, and tourists walked along the sidewalks. He walked around to the other side of the building. A staircase led up to a second floor.

"It's just upstairs." He jogged up the steps, pulling out a set of keys to unlock the door. When he opened the door, she heard noises from inside. He froze in the doorway, slamming the door closed before she could peek inside. "Holy —"

"What?" She poked her head around him, trying to see inside. "Are there rodents?"

"You could say that." His face turned a lighter shade of white as he stood there, not moving from the door. He covered his mouth with his hand.

Movement from inside made her look again, and she could hear people's voices, a man's and a woman's. Two almost naked figures ran around, collecting clothes off the floor.

He looked behind him into the window again. "I think it's best if I show you the apartment later."

"I thought you said it was empty?"

"Usually it is, but it seems that my brother's wife is using it for the time being."

"Your brother's wife?" Finally, Rachael got a look inside and recognized the man's face. "Isn't that …?"

"Yup. That's the jerk from last night." Jack's face was turning red. "That would be Freddy Harrington, the third."

"We should look for the dog."

He looked at her like she was crazy. "What?"

She almost couldn't believe she suggested it, either. Now that it was out there though, she figured if she didn't take him looking for the dog, something worse might happen than having to hang out with him a bit longer. He dropped his hand from the door handle.

"You want to look for the dog? With me?"

"We should call the shelters to see if anyone's missing a dog."

He looked in the window again. The two figures were now talking to one another, rushing around the room. "You know what, that actually sounds like a great idea. I have a buddy down at the police station."

"Let's start with the shelters." She didn't want to be around the police.

Just as he stepped down the stairs, his attention was stolen by the man's voice from inside the apartment and the door swung open. The woman ran barefoot down the steps toward Jack. She caught up to him as soon as he reached the bottom.

"Jack! Please, wait!" Panic filled her voice. She clasped her hands together as he turned to face her.

"You're sleeping with Freddy Harrington, Justine?" He didn't wait for her to answer. "How could you do that to Matt?"

"You don't know what our marriage has been like." She flung her finger in his face. Rachael's heart suddenly raced. A cold sweat formed at her hairline. She wanted to get away from the situation unfolding before her. She started to walk away without knowing where she was going. Anywhere but here.

"You need to talk to your husband, before I do," she heard him say from behind her. "Rachael, wait up!"

His footsteps turned into a jog as he caught up to her.

"You still want to look for that dog?" he asked.

She stopped and looked back at the woman standing in the middle of the road. Her chest heaved up and down as she focused on Jack. When Freddy came out of the apartment and walked down the stairs, he was fully dressed.

The woman ran toward Jack and Rachael in her bare feet. "Jack, please, we need to talk about this."

Freddy didn't appear upset at all. He swept back his hair. "Look Jack, you don't need to get involved in this."

Rachael noticed Jack's fist tense up.

"Stay off my property," Jack warned him.

"Looks like we interrupted his own plans for the apartment," Freddy smirked as he said this.

"Please, Jack, please understand," the woman sounded desperate.

"Go find your husband, before I do."

"Let's get out of here, Justine." Freddy pulled her back toward him by her elbow. Justine stumbled backwards, looking at them, her eyes wide. She didn't go back up to retrieve her things, instead, the two walked away down the road, out of sight.

Jack's fist loosened, but his eyes stayed on Justine and Freddy as they walked off.

"You okay?" Rachael asked.

He nodded, saying nothing at first, just kept his eyes on the retreating couple. When they were out of sight, he said, "How about we check the apartment out tomorrow?"

Worry trickled through her like water coming from a hose. What if he changes his mind and offers it to someone who can actually afford a place on the ocean? Where would she go then? "Do you mind if we still check the place out now?"

He looked surprised. "You want to go in there after all of that?"

"I would really appreciate it."

He gave her a look over, unsure. "Okay, no problem."

He walked back toward the restaurant, climbing up the stairs. She couldn't help but notice his perfectly worn jeans from behind. No full-blooded woman, no matter what her circumstances, could deny Jack's good looks and charisma, but she would never get involved with another man again.

He opened the door, but held out his hand, like he was stopping traffic. "Give me a minute."

He disappeared into the apartment as she walked to the length of the deck that ran along the back end of the restaurant. Rachael couldn't believe the place was for rent. She peeked through the window. Jack ran around the room, opening all the windows, grabbing the sheets and blankets and pulling them off.

"Go inside and check the place out," he said, as he descended the stairs with a ball of sheets in his hands.

She hesitated at first, glancing over her shoulder at the whole Atlantic Ocean sitting in front of her. The low tide revealed a seaweed-covered, rocky coast that curved slightly inward, like a waning moon. She covered her mouth with her hands, hiding a smile. She tiptoed inside as though she had to be careful or the whole place would fall apart beneath her feet. She stopped in the middle turning in a circle.

Jack leaned against the doorframe. "So, what do you think?"

She moved to the kitchen, opening up a cabinet door, checking inside, even though she wasn't looking for anything in particular. Next, she peeked inside the bathroom, flipping on the light. Inside there was a small stand-up shower, sink and toilet. She came out just as a flock of seagulls flew by the window. She watched as they floated in the air. "I'll take it."

He immediately smiled. "Great."

With his nails, he pried open the ring to his keys, twisted off a brass key and handed it over to her. He gestured his chin toward the living room. "So, the couch obviously pulls out and there's silverware, pots and pans in the kitchen. I'll grab some sheets and blankets for you, and a lot of disinfectant."

She shook her head. "I can go buy my own stuff."

"Where?" He shook his head. "It's Sunday. Nothing's open. It won't be a problem."

"Thanks, but I'm fine, really." She gave him a half smile, but she didn't want to be more indebted to him.

"There's a phone hooked up to the wall over there." He pointed to the kitchen. "The fire extinguisher is under the sink. Baking soda in the fridge." He pulled his phone from his pocket. "I've got to take this," he said, "but I'll come back with those sheets."

Of all the times in her life, why'd she have to meet a nice guy like Jack now?

CHAPTER 4

*R*achael held her hands behind her so Jack couldn't give back the money she had handed him.

"I don't want your money. You can pay me at the end of the month, when you're settled."

"No."

He eyed her, holding the cash in his hand. "You can pay at the end of the month."

"Rents are due at the beginning."

"You're seriously the most stubborn person I've ever met." He reached for his wallet and put the cash inside. "I'll be back with that lock."

"It's really okay." His generosity made her uncomfortable. "You don't have to go out of your way."

"I should've put a deadbolt in years ago." He rested his hands on his hips and looked around the room. "I can install it after I go to the hardware store, but in the meantime…" Jack pulled a business card from his wallet and wrote down a number. "This is my cell, in case you need anything."

She grabbed the card and held it up. Jack Williams, Executive Chef, The Fish Market.

"Executive Chef."

He stuffed his wallet in his back pocket. "Yup."

She held up the card. "Thanks."

"You're welcome." He hesitated for a second, looking as though he wanted to say something more, but then opened the door.

With a quick wave Jack left, and she watched him walk toward his truck in the parking lot and had to remind herself no matter how charming, she shouldn't trust him. When he was out of sight, she spun in a circle in the middle of the apartment, hugging herself, trying to hold onto the feeling she had at that moment.

Her own place to call home.

Right then, more than anything, she wished she could call her mother. Tell her about the view in front of her. Tell her about Finn, and how she was working a shift in a couple of hours.

She pulled out her phone and looked at her mom's number.

It wouldn't be worth it. She'd complain she left. What did she have to be ungrateful for? She had a man who wanted to stick around. Unlike her father, her mother would say.

She stuffed the phone in her back pocket and checked the place out. The wood floors creaked under her feet. She never had her own place before. A place where she could do what she wanted. Watch what she wanted. Play whatever music she wanted. Decorate the way she wanted.

She couldn't wait to get back to the hotel and grab the rest of her things, and check out.

"Do you need any toiletries or towels?" Henry asked as he handed over extra toothpaste, shampoo and conditioner, and a hug.

"I'm fine."

Henry shoved a box of donuts in her hands. "Come back if you do. No one's using them, you might as well."

"Thank you, Henry." Rachael gave him a hug.

"Don't even worry about it." He patted her back. "So, you're moving above the restaurant? You know, that Jack Williams is my nephew."

Rachael shook her head. "He is?"

"Every single woman in Camden Cove has tried to hook that one, but…maybe…?"

Rachael knew what the man was suggesting.

"Maybe all it takes is a newcomer." He winked at her.

Rachael had no business thinking about Jack Williams as more than her new landlord. "Goodbye, Henry."

"You be safe, and don't let that old grump Finn McCabe get under your skin."

Rachael laughed, then left and raced back to the apartment. The afternoon sun had crept behind the trees, sending long shadows against the pavement. A loud pop from a car's exhaust shot out, and an image of Nick flashed in her head. Her heart raced, and she felt light-headed. She walked to a tree, grabbing the rough bark to steady herself.

She still didn't know how he figured out her plan. She hadn't told anyone, not even her mother. She mulled it over, never writing down a thing, repeating it over and over in her head, so she wouldn't forget the details. How he figured it out frightened her more than Nick himself.

She climbed the steps to her new home, and checking over her shoulder the whole time, making sure no one had followed her or hid behind the dumpster. Her chest tightened as she unlocked the door, and only when the door clicked behind her was she able to take a deep breath. The excitement of her freedom was overshadowed by her fear of being found.

The sun lowered further in the sky, casting a golden hue throughout the space. Off in the distance, seagulls rested on the granite boulders at the water's edge. Memories she hadn't thought about in years flooded back. Memories of going to the beach as a kid. That was the happiest time in her life. They had been a family back then. Before he came back to get them, before he lost his job, and before he started drinking. On the weekends,

Finn took her by the hand and walked all the way down to the beach where the rocks made tide pools. He'd let her explore inside the tiny crevices and climb along the barnacle-covered rocks. When she found something, he'd hold it in his hand for her, and she'd examine the sea creature. The mystical beings of the ocean, right at her fingertips.

A seagull floated out to sea, its wings forming a V as it reached up toward the sky.

"Everything will be okay," she whispered to herself.

Without warning, a tear came loose and fell onto her chin. She quickly wiped it away, focusing on the room. The space wasn't very big, maybe the size of her living room back home in Rhode Island, but it would be hers.

Only hers.

She would be okay.

Jack stopped at the docks to find Matt's boat docked and empty. He swung by his house, but no one answered the door. He texted and called to no avail. In the meantime, he decided to stop at the hardware store and buy a new lock.

When he pulled into his driveway, Matt's truck was parked in front of the garage. He didn't see him until he walked out onto the deck in the back yard, sitting in one of his Adirondack chairs with a six-pack on the table next to him.

"I would've texted, but I wanted to be alone." Matt didn't look at him, just stared off at the horizon.

Jack patted Matt's back before sitting down in the other chair and grabbing one of the beers, twisting off the cap. "So, you've talked to Justine?"

Matt nodded and took a sip of his beer. "Yup."

"You okay?"

"I will be."

"Did you know?"

"I had a suspicion." Matt shrugged. "She got a bracelet for her birthday from someone anonymous. It was pretty expensive." Matt sighed. "At the time, I didn't know it was Freddy."

Jack should've hit Freddy. He had always undercut Matt throughout their childhood and now, even as an adult, he couldn't stop competing with him, with the fishing, the territories, the bull that went with it all. But no matter what Freddy's part was in all of this, nothing compared to the betrayal Justine had made. He knew better than anyone.

"Don't tell mom about any of this."

"Are you serious? You can't keep anything a secret in this town."

"Don't tell her anything, I mean it, Jack." Matt's tone said he meant business. "I don't need her knowing any more than she needs to. She already hates Justine."

"Why keep protecting her?"

"Because Justine and I have been through a lot together."

Jack held up his hands. He hadn't forgotten the year his brother had had. The shotgun wedding, the miscarriage, the nights they spent away from one another. The relationship had been doomed from the start. "She could've used a different place to sleep with Freddy."

"Well, she obviously wanted me to find out somehow."

"What was she thinking, sleeping with him?" The thought made him nauseous.

"Dude, stop reminding me."

"What are you going to do?"

"I don't know yet."

Jack almost said something sarcastic, but instead let out a sigh. "How are you staying so flipping rational?"

"I had a feeling it was going to happen sooner or later. I didn't cheat on her, but I didn't act much like a husband, either." Matt took another drink. "She's having Freddy move in."

"Are you kidding me?" Jack did a double take. "She kicked you out?"

"Let's just say I didn't take the news too well."

"You should've thrown her stuff out the window."

"Jack, I don't need you to give me advice on this."

Jack held up his hands. Matt was right. "Do you need help with moving?"

"I was sort of hoping for the apartment above the restaurant."

"Sorry." Jack shook his head.

"What?" Matt's jaw dropped. "I thought the place was empty?"

"Because that's where your wife was sleeping with another man, that's why." Jack couldn't even imagine Matt wanting to live there.

"She probably slept with him in my house, too," he argued. "Probably even on my boat! She obviously used all her resources."

"Look, I just rented it out to someone." Jack took a sip of his beer. He hoped Jack wouldn't ask.

"Who?" Matt suddenly looked angry.

"A woman who just moved to town." Jack focused on the water in front of him.

"The waitress?" Matt's eyes widened. "You're choosing a stranger over your own brother! Whose wife slept with Freddy Harrington?! I'll just give you the two hundred dollars."

"Now you're upset?" Jack almost laughed, but stopped himself when he saw Matt's face flash red.

"I'm upset, because I just learned that not only did my wife cheat on me, but I'm homeless unless I live with my mom and dad." Matt put his head between his hands. "It seriously can't get worse than this."

"It sounds really bad when you put it like that," Jack said, "but you can stay at my place for as long as you want."

"Stay here?" This offer didn't seem to make things better. "I don't want to stay here. Not that I have many options right now." Matt's shoulders fell forward. "I'll just stay on my boat."

Jack shook his head. "You don't want to stay out there, not with winter coming. Stay here. It'll be like old times, except we won't have to share a room."

"So who is this woman?"

"Her name is Rachael and she needs the apartment."

"Is there more to this woman?" he asked.

Jack didn't know for sure. "I have this feeling she's running away from some sort of trouble."

"And you're sure *she* isn't the trouble?" Matt shook his head, staring him down. "Take it from me, you never really know a person. Be careful."

Jack nodded. "Is there anything I can do?"

"There's one thing." Matt stood up. "Can you deal with mom?"

"What do you mean?"

"If Freddy's moving into my house," he opened the sliding glass door, "you know all of them are going to be calling in a matter of minutes."

Suddenly, Jack's phone dinged, vibrating in his pocket. Elizabeth's name flashed across the screen.

Call me!

How did she hear about it? She was on her honeymoon!

"Thanks, man." Matt walked into the house, leaving Jack with his phone now ringing. His uncles' number flashed across the screen. It would be only a matter of time before it would be his mom. He pulled his keys out of his front pocket and walked to his truck. He'd head over to his parents' house to tell Sarah in person, before the gossip train hit her.

When he pulled up, Sarah stood on the side porch that led to the kitchen.

"What's going on with Matt?" she asked as soon as he opened the truck's door.

"Let's go inside." He had loved growing up in this neighborhood, kids everywhere, with houses close to one another. It made for great games of kick-the-can and ghost around the house. But the number one neighborhood rule was that family secrets were told inside.

She followed him in, wringing a dish towel in her hand. Once the door slammed shut, she began, "Margie told Frank that someone saw Matthew leaving his house with a bag of stuff, and Freddy Harrington's car has been parked there all day. I've tried getting hold of him, but you know how he is with answering his phone." She continued without taking a breath as Jack stood there in the doorway. "Your father and I drove down to see what was going on." She pointed to his dad, sitting in his recliner. "And sure as the name on my birth certificate, there's Freddy Harrington's sports car parked out front."

Without saying a word, Jack ushered his mother to her seat at the kitchen table, pulled out the chair, and helped her sit down.

"Is he okay?" She grabbed his arm, her eyes full of worry.

"Yes... and no." He walked to the coffee maker and scooped out fresh grounds from the tin can, enough for a full pot. John got out of his recliner and moved to his seat at the table next to Sarah, patting her hand. Jack leaned against the counter and faced his parents as the coffee percolated. "It looks like the marriage might be over."

Sarah let out a gasp, though Jack was fairly certain she had already come to that conclusion.

"He'll get through this." John leaned over to Sarah, rubbing her shoulder. "The one thing about Matt that you can always count on, is his strength."

The coffee spurted and sputtered. Jack wondered what he would've done if Rachael hadn't been there. He'd probably wind up having to hire a lawyer. That was the kind of fighter Freddy was, a guy who paid his attorney fees.

"Something must've been going on for a while." His mother clasped her hands together on the table. "What do you know?"

"Not much." He shook his head. "I hate to admit that I'm not sorry it's over." At least, Jack hoped as much. He was secretly glad Justine finally got caught, especially after that night last summer. He couldn't wait for her to be out of their lives forever.

"How long has this affair with Freddy been going on?"

"We need to stay out of it, mom."

Sarah's fingers blazed across the screen of her phone. He

could only imagine what his sisters and uncles were texting back. There was most likely a group text going on at this point. "There was something about that girl from the beginning, when she pretended to be Elizabeth's friend, sneaking into this house just so she could get close to Matt."

"Mom, that was high school."

John pointed his finger in the air. "Thank God she didn't get pregnant again."

Would children have made the difference for the two of them? Jack shook his head. No. Children, he was sure, would have made no difference.

For another hour his mom continued to ask questions, but Jack kept telling her the same things, over and over. No, he didn't know what was going on. No, it wasn't their business. And it was Matt who needed to decide what to do. If he wanted them to stay out of it, then that's what they needed to do to support him.

Sarah's phone vibrated against the table. She picked it up and read the message. "Your brother is staying with you?"

"Matt's now responding?" Jack let out a sigh. "Yes."

Sarah looked at him over her reading glasses. "What about the apartment above the restaurant?"

Not this again. "I already found an occupant."

"Who?"

"A woman who's new to town."

"The woman who came to the restaurant during the wedding?" She gave him that look of hers she gave when she thought he was making a mistake.

Did anyone see Rachael the way he did? "She was looking for a place to rent."

Sarah sighed, shaking her head. "I just cannot believe Justine snuck around with Freddy, of all people."

"Please don't make this a big deal."

"Make what a big deal?" Sarah acted innocent, but she knew what Jack was talking about.

"Matt and Justine."

"Listen to the boy, Sarah," John said. "Matt doesn't want you getting involved in this."

"Well, we stayed out of his marriage, and look where that got us." Sarah pointed her phone at the both them. "I think I can take it from here."

Jack shook his head as his sister Lauren swung open the kitchen door, rushing into the house.

"Where is he?" she asked, dropping her purse onto the counter and headed straight to the table.

"Well, he's homeless right now." Sarah shrugged her shoulders. "So we don't really know."

"We do know." He couldn't believe how dramatic his mom was being. He spoke directly to Sarah, "He's at *my* place."

"Can't he just stay at the apartment?" His younger sister swayed her neck to one side, the way she did when she was a teenager and about to get sassy, as his mom liked to call it. Jack had a completely different word for it, but he was a gentleman.

"I rented it out." Jack picked up his mug and got up from the table, knowing what Lauren was about to say next.

"You rented it out? To who?" Lauren's eyebrow perked up.

"To that woman at the wedding," Sarah said.

"The woman who was dripping wet?" Lauren made a face.

"Don't you two want to talk about Justine?" he asked, desperate to change the subject.

"Not until you tell us who this girl is."

Didn't they need to focus their attention on the real villain? Not the new woman in town? Jack dumped his coffee in the sink and waved to his family. "I have to go home and get my guest room prepared."

He patted his dad on the back, gave his sister a hug and then kissed his mom on the cheek.

"Tell him to just come home," she said, holding onto him.

"He can stay at your house," John protested. "We still have Lauren."

"Thanks, Dad." Lauren rolled her eyes.

"John!" Sarah's eyes bulged. "This is our children's home, always."

"He's fine, mom, really." Jack opened the door. He couldn't wait to get out of there. "He just wants to be left alone."

As do I.

Lauren put her hands on her hips. "Sorry we care."

Jack gave her a look. "I know you do."

He didn't want his brother to get dragged through the mud, but watching his family rally together pulled at his heart strings.

It's what the Williamses did. They protected each other.

Rachael found a tea kettle in the oven and filled it under the faucet. While she waited for it to heat up, she spun the couch to face the windows and sat staring out. The afternoon sun had deep shades of pink and orange casting off the clouds over the blackened sea. The scene made her forget her problems for a just a second.

When the kettle screamed, she went back to reality and back to her problems. She sat at the table, pulling out her things from her bag and shuffling through them. She counted out her money, like she did every night, and put it back into her wallet. She wanted to buy a car. A car could also be a shelter for her, if worst came to worst. Inside a plastic bag, she had all of Rachael Milano's information — her driver's license, her credit cards, and all her other documents.

Nicholas Milano's wife.

She wanted to go back to Rachael Hawkins, the girl who believed in herself.

Would she be able to find her in Camden Cove? Or was she gone forever?

The answer? She didn't know. The person in the photos staring back at her seemed so different than the person she was today. If she could be thankful for one thing, it was she wasn't that person anymore.

When she noticed the time, she jumped up, scraping the chair against the floor. She needed to be at Finn's in less than a half hour. Gathering her things, she went to the fridge and grabbed a frozen pizza from the previous tenant and dumped it in the garbage. She stuffed her money and information inside the cardboard box and put it back inside. That would have to be her bank until she figured out what to do. Not like she could go to a bank. If she set up an account, she'd need an I.D. If she used her current one then her information, her address, all of that would be out there. Nick would be able to find her if he looked.

Was she crazy?

Maybe now that she's gone, he's happy she left.

Maybe all this running was for nothing.

Maybe.

CHAPTER 5

*R*achael slept through the night from the day she moved into the apartment. And each morning, she gave thanks to be waking up to the waves and the seagull's cry. Even though most mornings the fog covered up the sunrise, she got out of bed just to see the earth waking up. The view never disappointed. Even on its worst day, the rocky shore impressed.

The coast of Rhode Island had been just as beautiful, but anyone who wanted to live on the water needed to have money in order to enjoy it. Never in a million years could she live in a place like this and be able to afford it on a waitress' salary. It occurred to her that she probably *couldn't* afford a place like this, even in the off season, like Jack tried to convince her. He probably low-balled the price, just so she'd agree to stay.

Why was he trying so hard to help her? What was in it for him?

Lying in bed, she didn't want to waste time contemplating it. She got up and dressed, so she could walk the trail. She had picked up a bag of dry dog food at the market. She'd go to the same spot she had been when the dog first approached her. He hadn't come from the trail, but from the water's edge. She guessed there might be some sort of shelter close by, as she had seen dog prints in the sand.

She didn't eat much breakfast, instead packing a little snack for her walk. She followed the gravel trail with her hands stuffed in her pockets. The foggy day had a bite to it when the wind picked up. She'd have to start thinking about buying some winter clothes and better shoes. She thought of her full closet of outfits she had left behind.

Most of the time, Nick loved to spoil her. He'd do anything for her.

Anything.

Nick was the first friend to offer a hand. The kind of guy who'd give the shirt he was wearing if someone needed it. The first to run into danger to protect. Nick was all of that. Sometimes he'd come home with expensive gifts he couldn't' afford "just to make her smile". However, the highs always came with the lows. And at the end, there were too many lows.

Off in the distance, Seagulls flew in the sky, calling out. The sun peeked out of the clouds, making the air suddenly heavy. It took everything she had to not look out at Jack's house up ahead. The permeating smell of beach roses lingered as she past the pink petals that lined the edge of his property. They were her favorite, as a kid. She'd pick the delicate roses and press them between the pages of her books.

Bushes and other trees covered up most of the property, obstructing the view from the trail. Only the second floor windows could be seen. The coast curved like a horseshoe at that point, mostly granite cliffs, but in between the rocks, small sandy beaches could be seen, especially with the tide out. Off in the distance, a mile or so away, a red and white lighthouse stood on an island.

The view was killer.

Then she thought about Nick's place when she first saw it, a beautiful home, in a family friendly neighborhood. Inside, he had new furniture. Everything looked nice. But nice things only covered up the dirt underneath for so long.

And everyone had dirt.

She continued walking down the trail to the small inlet, where the dog had been the day before, then climbed down the rocks, holding onto the small bag of food. The black dog had been a good size, probably over sixty pounds, but looked like he hadn't eaten a regular meal in weeks. As she looked around for any sign, she peeked around some rocks and couldn't believe her eyes. The dog sat on the beach, looking out at the water.

He startled when she gasped, but he didn't run. Rachael pulled out some of the kibble and put it down in front of her, stepping back to give him some space. The dog slowly got up, keeping his eyes on her. She tensed up, trying to stay as still as possible as he approached the food.

"That's a good boy," she said, her voice soft. "Come and get it."

He sniffed the ground around the kibble, gobbled up the pieces in one bite, then looked up at her. She set out some more food, and stepped back again, but not as far. He came closer, scarfed it down, then looked up at her, waiting for more. This time she knelt, placed the kibble in her palm, and held it out for him.

"Come on, little man, you don't have to be afraid." She held her hand steady.

He came forward slowly, stretching out his neck. His nose sniffed the kibble's scent in the air. He scooted forward, but was still too far away to snatch it out of her hand. She wasn't worried that he would bite her. His gentle nature, even when hungry, proved he didn't want to hurt anyone. He was just frightened and lost.

Then, as if he decided to go for it, he walked up, sat down at her feet and ate the kibble from her palm. Rachael refilled it, and he stayed where he was, watching her scoop the food into her hand. After four more scoops, all of the food was gone, and the dog licked off the remnants.

He looked up at her when her hand was good and clean. His big brown eyes spoke the thanks she knew he was trying to tell her. Then he licked her face, and she laughed. She reached out to pet him and he jumped back, but only a little. Slowly, she extended her hand to his neck and scratched under his thick coat. He leaned into her hand as she dug around the matted fur.

He wore no collar, and from his size she was sure he wasn't a puppy, but he wasn't much older than a year or so. "Do you like to play?"

His head cocked.

She picked up a stick, throwing it toward the water. He didn't move.

"Guess not." She went back to scratching him. He stood up as she reached his rear end, and when she found a spot on his back leg, he began licking her hand as she continued to scratch.

"Where are you from?" she asked aloud, as though he could understand. He suddenly fell to the ground and rolled over, showing his belly.

How could she, of all people, help this dog? She could barely help herself. She could bring him to the apartment. Give him more food, then call the shelters. Maybe take him to a vet. Would Jack be okay with her having a dog in the apartment?

She grabbed the belt she had packed and looped it through the buckle, gradually moving towards the dog's neck. He flipped over just as she made her way toward his head. She froze, but it was too late. He jumped up, taking off before she came close enough to get a hold of him.

He ran down the beach, heading toward town. She got up, grabbed her things, and ran after him as fast as she could, but the rocks and waves soon washed away his footprints. What if he got stuck when the tide came in?

Jack ran up the apartment steps with a gift bag in his hand. That morning, he'd gone for his usual run. With some dog food, he ran down the trail, half expecting, half hoping to run into the dog. He didn't expect to run into Rachael again. But there she was on the trail. The waves covered the sound of his footsteps this time, and he watched as she knelt in front of the dog as he rolled on his back, completely open to her presence. In one of her hands, she had a belt and she tried to wrangle it around his neck. She almost had him, too, but the dog spooked and took off.

Rachael followed the dog and he decided to give her some space. The last thing he wanted was to weird her out more by showing up again where she happened to be. So he continued his run, then headed over to his sister Elizabeth's clinic to pick up a few things — a leash, a few toys, and a collar.

Now back from her honeymoon, Elizabeth had been filled in on the situation with Justine and Freddy. "And you gave the apartment to someone else?"

"Does anyone else understand the law?" Jack came to the realization his family was all crazy.

"Maybe instead of taking in strays, you should focus on your family." It hit below the belt, but Jack knew she was only protecting Matt, who now slept in 400-count Egyptian cotton sheets on a queen-sized bed.

"He's going to be okay." Most nights ended with the two brothers sitting in Jack's living room, watching a game. Matt had been upset, but he had also confessed that he felt relief when Justine told him it was over. Jack wondered if Matt knew about last summer, but he didn't ask. He'd be pouring salt into a wound, and he wasn't sure Matt would recover from that one.

"How could she sleep with Freddy Harrington of all people?" Elizabeth's true anger surfaced. "It's like she purposely chose the one guy who'd get the most under Matt's skin."

"The whole marriage was a mistake." Jack didn't need to analyze it any more than he already had. The only reason Matt and Justine hurried into marriage was because she got pregnant.

When Justine lost the baby, it was only a matter of time. If he was truly being honest, he wasn't shocked when he saw Justine in the apartment that day. He just thought she'd have enough decency to break it off, rather than explode it into pieces. But maybe Matt was right. Maybe that was her way of getting his attention. She certainly had a way of getting *everyone's* attention.

Elizabeth handed him a chew toy and asked, "What's going on with you and this new girl?"

"What?" He gave his sister a look, adjusting his baseball cap. "Nothing."

"Seriously?" She waited for him to say more, but when he didn't, said, "Tell Matt he can stay at the farm."

Elizabeth's farm was the last place a guy whose marriage just fell apart would want to stay. The perfect newlyweds. Adam and Elizabeth were the annoying couple who finished each other's sentences and laughed at their own inside jokes. There was no way he'd tell him to go to the farm.

She must have read his thoughts, because she added, "Just tell him, Jack."

"Fine, I'll tell him." He grabbed the dog stuff and kissed his sister on the cheek. "How are you feeling, Mrs. Cahill?"

"I'm happy."

He nodded, but had no idea what he should tell his sister because he was the last person who understood love. "I'm happy for you."

She rolled her eyes, then kissed him on the cheek. "Tell him I love him."

He kissed her back. "I will."

When he returned to the restaurant, he put all the dog stuff in an extra gift bag he found and stood at Rachael's door with it in his hand. He knocked on the glass, but turned away from the window, making sure he didn't look inside the apartment. He figured she probably wouldn't be cool with him peeking through the windows, even with good intentions. After a minute he knocked again, but heard nothing. She either wasn't home or didn't want to answer. He left the bag on the doorknob and went back down to the restaurant. The shipment for his paper supplies was coming in, and he needed to finish the new month's schedule.

He looked forward to fall's slower pace and winter's break. The restaurant would stay open until New Year's, then he planned to close it down and take off. He didn't know where, but somewhere. Last year, he promised he'd leave, but with the renovations, he stayed put. Not this year. Maybe he'd convince Matt to take off with him. They could go somewhere warm, sit on a beach. Then an image of Rachael in a bathing suit, sitting on a beach next to him, popped in his head.

He shook it away as he walked out of his office and into the kitchen. This is where Jack thrived. He had two cooks on the line that night. Even though the tourist season had come to an end for most in Camden Cove, The Fish Market still thrived. People didn't mind the drive to the small town for a dinner on the water.

He walked the floor, checking on things before heading back to the kitchen. Orders came in and out efficiently. Everything seemed under control, but something inside of Jack felt very much out of control.

He opened the back door to see if the bag was still on the doorknob, but stopped himself just in time. Maybe she hadn't even come home yet. He shook his head and shut the door. Nope. He gave her the present because of the dog. It wasn't about him. She clearly had a way with the dog, and she could help him if she had the right tools.

"You're losing it," he whispered to himself as he shook his head and walked back inside. His sous chef gave him a look.

"You okay, man?"

Jack wasn't, but like he really wanted to talk about his feelings about a woman who was still a complete mystery. "Yeah, fine."

He left before Michael could say something back, heading to his office before he did something else stupid. He wasn't fine, at all.

Rachael's feet pounded and her back ached as she walked back to the apartment from another shift at the tavern, but she relished it. A hard day's work felt good. Her body liked pushing itself. She had always enjoyed the busyness of waiting tables, keeping the customers happy. She liked listening to their stories. People would tell her about their day, or how they felt about the news, or talk endlessly about the weather. She noticed how almost every conversation circled back to the water somehow.

She had met Nick working at a restaurant downtown Providence. He worked nights then, and had come in to help with an ambulance. The handsome officer impressed her right away with the way he carried himself in the situation.

The next day, flowers sat on top of the front counter for her with a card asking her out for dinner and she called him right then. He took her all the way in Newport, eating along the water, then driving around looking at the mansions, imagining what it would be like to live there.

They talked all night. He told her about growing up, and wanting to be a cop. He listened as she explained how she worked to pay for college. She had thought he was sweet when he told her he would get her to marry him one day. That was the first sign of his control and she totally missed it.

During the day, the tavern usually didn't have much business, but for some reason it was pretty crowded. She did great in tips. Locals were starting to recognize her. The old timers called her "sweetie" or "hon", but she didn't mind, as long as their tips were as sweet as well.

Everyone seemed to be in a good mood, too, because even Finn told her to take the night off, then he invited her to dinner.

"Sunday night," he huffed. "I make a pot roast at five."

"You're inviting me over?" She almost jumped up and hugged him, but held back. "What can I bring?"

"Something green, I guess."

Heading down Harbor Lane, a bell from a lobster boat rang out, drawing her back into the present. That's when she noticed something hanging on the door. A bag. Something Nick would do after he lost his temper. A 'sorry' gift. Her heart pounded as she stopped halfway up the stairs. She immediately checked her surroundings. Could he be hiding behind the dumpster? Or around the side of the restaurant, near the main road? Could he be hiding over toward the water, or on the trail? Was he already inside? There were too many places to hide, and she felt completely exposed. Should she run, leave her things behind and go?

She slowly climbed the steps, keeping an eye out for movement below her. From the window, everything inside looked exactly like it did when she left. All the lights were still on, and all the doors left open. Trembling, she grabbed the bag and looked inside.

A dog collar?

She pulled out a black leash, and underneath she saw a few plastic dog toys. There was also a handwritten note.

Thought you might need this next time.

Jack

Had he been watching her? Following her from afar?

Without going inside, she pounded down the stairs, walking straight into the restaurant kitchen.

"Where's Jack?" She directed her question to the first person she saw.

A young cook pointed down a hallway at the other side of the kitchen. She didn't even slow down, just walked right down toward the hall when Jack came walking out.

"Were you following me?" She pushed the bag into his chest. The staff stopped moving and watched. Jack looked around, clearly horrified, but she didn't care. He had crossed the line.

"I went for a run, like I do every day, at the same time I do every day." He spoke slowly and calmly, which irritated her, because she wasn't calm at all. "You happened to be there again."

"Then you say hello, instead of watching me. What's with you and sneaking around?"

"I saw you from far away, I wasn't sneaking around. I didn't want to scare the dog again, and make *you* mad again." He stopped and shook his head. "I'm sorry. You were trying to grab him, and then you ran after him. I thought it'd be weirder if I ran after you."

The staff lost interest and moved on to what they had been doing before she stormed into the restaurant.

"I feel like a broken record, but next time you should let someone know you're there."

"You hungry?" he asked, changing the subject as he passed the bag back to her.

"Excuse me?" This wasn't over, as far as she was concerned.

"We're about to start service, and I have these sample meals left over." He pointed to a few dishes on the counter. A white-crusted fish sat perfectly plated next to another dish was filled with pasta and thick chucks of lobster in a creamy white sauce. He eyed her.

"You still upset?" He pushed a dish closer to her.

She pushed it back. "I don't want your charity."

"Believe me, I know." His eyebrows lifted as his attention was stolen by a waitress.

"A couple wants to change their order, but Michael's basically done with the meal." Jack nodded and held up his finger at Rachael, then he and the waitress headed toward the cook, leaving Rachael behind.

Rachael wasn't sure if she was going to storm out of the restaurant or poke that finger right back at him. She certainly wasn't going to grab that plate of food, no matter how delicious it smelled. A waitress stepped up, taking one of them off the counter.

Rachael stepped aside, bumping into a cook. "Coming or going?"

"Going." Rachael turned around, walking through kitchen and out the back.

As she made her way up the stairs to her apartment, she heard a woman's voice call out.

"Hey!"

Rachael turned around. The waitress held out a to-go box. "Jack wants you to have this."

"Tell him, I'm good." She held her hand up. "But thanks."

"Seriously, here." The woman reached it out further. "You know, Jack's a really nice guy. I'd take the meal."

Reluctantly, Rachael stepped down and took it. Her stomach growled at the aroma drifting from inside. The waitress scooted back into the restaurant, slamming the screen door shut behind. From inside, she heard Jack call out an order to the staff.

Looking at the container in her hands, she climbed back up, popped off the top and sniffed the dish. The creamy aroma reminded her of the night she came into town. Maybe if she wanted the dog to accept her generosity, she'd have to be willing to accept some herself. Wasn't that the way things worked?

CHAPTER 6

*W*hen Finn reminded her of dinner, she felt embarrassed, but had to ask for a ride.

"You don't have a car?" He seemed shocked. "How have you been getting around?"

"I walk." The apartment above The Fish Market had been a blessing. She could get all the essentials from the Country Store, and she couldn't afford extras, anyways.

Finn instructed her to be ready at quarter to five on the dot. "I don't appreciate anyone wasting my time."

So, five minutes before he was supposed to come, she waited at the bottom of the apartment steps with a salad and mint chocolate chip ice cream. She wasn't sure if it was just her childhood memories blending into her dreams, but thought she remembered that Finn liked that flavor.

Rachael jumped when the restaurant's screen door slammed shut.

"Sorry, I didn't mean to startle you." Jack looked up from his phone, clearly not expecting to see her.

"No, it's fine," she said, suddenly feeling awkward from their last encounter.

She hadn't seen much of Jack. He was definitely avoiding her, after she flipped out on the poor guy. She winced at the thought.

He stood as autumn leaves cascaded to the ground from the trees in the parking lot. Her mother had always told her the falling of the leaves was nature's way of letting go of the past. She wished she could shed her past, grow again and start anew, but her roots were too deep, too scarred.

"You going to a Congregational church's potluck?" he asked, pointing at the containers in her hands.

She smiled, about to answer, when Finn pulled into the parking lot. "I'm having dinner."

"With Finn?" Jack appeared amused.

"Yes." Rachael opened the passenger door and got in as Jack walked over to the driver's side. Finn rolled down the window and the men shook hands.

"How's it going?"

"Good." Finn tilted his head toward her. "Glad you were able to rent Rachael your place."

"The apartment was sitting empty, so I was glad to find someone to fill it."

"Heard your brother's staying at your place." Finn hadn't spoken this much since she came to town. "Shame about his wife."

Jack stuffed his hands in his pockets. "Well, it is what it is."

Finn nodded at the vague statement. "True."

Jack's eyes darted from Finn to Rachael, not hiding his curiosity. But Finn didn't gratify it before saying, "Have a good one," and rolled up his window.

As they arrived at Finn's, Rachael realized that her memories of the house had been more dream than reality. Stepping inside, everything seemed a lot smaller than she remembered. The screened porch had seemed huge when she was little, but it only fit a couple of chairs. The kitchen, which she'd thought ran the whole length of the house, sat in the back and was quite small. But his bedroom was off the living room like she remembered, and a small staircase led up from the dining room to her mother's bedroom.

The table had been set, and there were even linen napkins.

"Hope you like pot roast." He set a Dutch oven onto the table and uncovered it. Steam rose up as she leaned over to look inside.

"It smells delicious." And it did.

She grabbed a plate at the head of the table and uncovered her salad. "Would you like some?"

Finn made a face, then shrugged. "Why not?"

He poured two glasses of water and sat down.

She sat down across from him, hoping a topic of conversation would pop into her mind.

"Tell me when," he said, scooping a huge portion of pot roast onto her plate.

"Thank you." She held up her hand. "That's enough for me."

"So, you're settled in, then?" he asked, doubling the portion on his own plate.

"Yes." She placed her napkin in her lap. "I really lucked out."

"Yeah, well, Jack's a good kid. I've known the Williamses for years. Good family." He chewed loudly as he spoke. "He really turned that place into something, since he took over."

"He should be the one staying in the apartment, with all the hours he puts in the restaurant."

"Always working, that one, since he was a little boy." Finn swallowed, then wiped his mouth with his napkin. "You knew that he was going places, even back then."

Rachael took a sip of her water, fighting an urge to find out more about Jack. He seemed perfect. Although, she had learned, no one is *really* perfect.

Her outburst on Jack flashed in her head. She had accused him of something terrible, and he didn't lose his temper even the slightest bit. If that had been Nick, she certainly wouldn't end up with food as the result. She had learned her lesson the one time she disagreed with him in front of his boss and his wife at the Christmas party. He had laughed it off in front of everyone. She didn't even know she had made him angry until they got in the car. He backhanded her so fast she had no time to react. Right behind her ear. The momentum of the blow propelled her face into the car's window. She hadn't even noticed the cut on the side of her head, because her breath had been ripped away.

"Oh god, oh god, Rachael," he kept repeating as he opened the glove box. She gasped for breath as he pulled out napkins from a fast food chain. He placed the whole stack on her eyelid, where she was cut. She still couldn't catch her breath. "Oh god. I'm so sorry, Rachael. I'm so sorry. Oh god."

She only reached for the door to get some air, but Nick pulled her hand away from the handle. Then held it closed. "You can't go out there. We will lose everything, if you go out there."

Her lungs cemented in place, the air wouldn't come. She had just wanted air to breathe.

As he drove her to the emergency room, he came up with the story. She had slipped on the ice. He mentioned that he was a cop, making connections between the hospital staff and the department. The doctor never even questioned a thing.

The next day, she went to her mother's. Nick begged for forgiveness, calling and coming to the house. Her mother all but sent her back, convincing her that he seemed genuine. Wasn't she lucky her husband wanted to stick around?

Nick really did seem genuine. Each day, he'd stop by with some new gift, or just to see her. He'd tell her how much he missed her, and how sorry he was. How he had been stressed with work. How it was an accident. He promised he'd never do it again.

He always promised.

Jack may be a genuinely nice guy, like the girl said, but if he only knew the half of Rachael's problems, he'd steer clear away. He probably dated those cute kind of girls. The teacher, the nurse, or the girl who filled her profile on Facebook with posts about how being a mom was her full-time job. His dream girl certainly wasn't homeless, broke, and clearly a bad judge of character.

"You going to tell your mother where you are?" Finn asked, in-between bites. "Not that it's any of my business."

She shrugged. "I don't really know."

She promised herself she wouldn't lie, no matter what, when it came to Finn.

He looked up at the ceiling, as though contemplating her answer. "I guess I believe a parent has a right to know if their child is okay or not."

She looked down at her plate, and picked at her meat with her fork. "I'm afraid she doesn't see my side of things."

He clicked his tongue, then scooped up a potato with his fork and knife. "I suppose she doesn't need to know."

She looked up, noticing that her second-grade photo was framed on the mantle. Her front teeth were missing. Freckles dotted her nose. That little girl was as more of a dream than reality.

She should call and let her mom know she was okay, but there was no doubt in her mind that Nick would go and talk with her. He'd beg her mom for forgiveness, promising the moon and the stars and the sky, groveling about his wrongdoing. He'd seem sincere. Maybe he would be. Or the other Nick, the one who could frighten criminals, might make her mother tell him everything she knew. Then, it wouldn't matter which Nick he was, because he'd come after her either way.

The rest of the dinner went on in silence. Finn wiped his plate clean with his last bite of roast and set his napkin on the table. "I'll clean up, and grab us some ice cream."

Rachael stood up, grabbing her dinner plate and glass. "Let me help."

He gave her a nod, then walked to the kitchen.

"This place looks the same." She couldn't believe it. The small kitchen lived up to her memories. It hadn't changed a bit. The same old wallpaper, discolored by time, was still on the walls. The stained glass lamp hung above the sink, and the biblical quotes, hand stitched by her grandmother, framed by the door.

"Don't need all those fancy gadgets you kids have nowadays."

The place had been kept clean. She was glad to see Finn took care of himself.

He scooped two bowls of ice cream as Rachael washed the dishes. He set them down on the small table in the kitchen. Again, silence fell over them as they ate their ice cream, but she didn't mind, much. She preferred not having to skirt around the truth.

He scraped the last remaining drops of mint chocolate chip from the bottom of his bowl and spooned it up. "You'll need something for the winter, and I need a new truck that I can do more deliveries. We might find a deal, it being the end of the season and all."

"What?"

"You can take my old truck until you find something."

"I can't take your truck."

"Sure you can."

She shook her head, stabbing her spoon into her ice cream. "I've saved enough to buy my own vehicle, but thanks."

"Well, you better do something soon, otherwise there'll be nothing left."

He got up and dumped his bowl into the sink. "I should probably take you home."

She looked down at her half-eaten ice cream. "Sure. That sounds good."

She took one last bite before Finn was at the door. She set the bowl in the sink, shaking her head. The man clearly hadn't hung out with people anywhere besides the bar in a while.

"Don't forget your salad." He pointed to her container. She grabbed it, then walked out behind him to his truck. She inspected it. It was practically new. *He had no use for a new truck.* His was just fine, but she appreciated his thoughtfulness.

When he pulled up to the apartment, he looked straight ahead, out the windshield.

"Thanks again for dinner," she said, the wind from the ocean blowing her hair across her face.

He nodded, waved quickly, and pulled off down the road. She watched as he drove away before going to the apartment. Once inside, she did her usual check. First the closets, then she shook the windows, then relocked them. She looked behind the shower curtain, then in the linen closet. When she finished her last check, she went to bed.

Sleep came at once, and she slept well, too. The ocean waves lulled her dreams and the nightmares stayed away for another night.

Morning came with a new energy and she flung her blankets back. With both arms, she threw open the curtains. The sun hit her face as it peeked over the horizon. A lobster boat floated out on the water. She watched as it slowly moved its way along the skyline until it disappeared.

As she ate her cereal, staring out at the water, her eyes continued to wander over toward the trail. She could just make out the part right before Jack's house. She kept telling herself that she wasn't trying to see it through the trees, but her eyes kept straining.

Why couldn't she stop thinking about him?

It was the fairytale complex. The knight in shining armor kind of thing her subconscious wanted. Or maybe it was the way he offered to help her out, or how he stood up for her, or that great smile of his.

She pushed her bowl away, the plastic-y taste of her bargain corn flakes getting to her. She grabbed a baggie and filled it with dog food, putting it in her backpack with the leash and collar Jack got her. She'd look for more work, any kind of job someone wanted to hire her for. At this point, the tavern wasn't cutting it, if she did want to buy a car.

She headed up Harbor Lane and stopped in the small pharmacy. The man said they weren't hiring. The next stop was a bakery, La Patisserie. As she stepped inside, the light, sweet, smell of confectioners' sugar encompassed her. Glass cases lined the back wall, filled with sweet delicacies. Cakes sat on glass stands, fruit tarts rested on linen napkins covering silver trays, with even more trays of croissants and eclairs and perfectly golden cream-puffs. Rachael wished she'd skipped the cornflakes as she reached the counter.

"What can I get for you this morning?" The man behind the counter leaned his arms against the case.

She hated this exact moment for so many reasons. Then, she bit the bullet and asked, "I was wondering if you were looking for any help?"

The man grimaced and shook his head. Her timing couldn't have been worse. Her plan ruined. She'd meant to leave for Camden Cove in the spring. Places would be hiring all the time, preparing for the busy tourist season. She'd be lost in the summer crowds. No one would notice the outsider during the summer. But in the fall, when there were no jobs, she stuck out. She was like those few roses still in bloom. People were waiting for you to disappear.

"No, unfortunately. Just not enough business this time of year."

She forced herself to smile. "Thanks, anyway."

"My nephew has a restaurant down the road, The Fish Market. Have you tried there?" he asked.

Of course, he'd recommend the one place she couldn't work. "Thanks."

She looked out at the display of pastries. Her stomach growled. The smell of the fresh roasted coffee made her pull out some cash. "Can I grab a small coffee and one of those chocolate croissants?"

The man smiled and nodded. "For here?"

Only an older couple sat in the middle of the floor, leaving the tables by the windows open. "Yes, please."

He grabbed the croissant, placed it on a plate, and handed her a coffee cup. "New in town?"

"Sort of." She shrugged, but didn't add any more. "Thanks."

"Welcome to Camden Cove," he said as he passed back her change. "Hope you find something."

She gave him a nod and turned to the coffee, pouring a dark brew into her mug. She crossed the room and sat facing the harbor. The empty street and the sunny autumn morning brought a tranquil feeling to the town. The water's surface was calm, sprinkled with red, yellow, and burnt orange leaves from the trees hanging along its edges. Only a few people walked the streets, just meandering, not hitting the shops.

At this point, she definitely didn't have enough money for a decent car. She pulled out the bus schedule she had picked up at the station and looked at the other routes she could take with what she had. She could get to Portland, but she wanted to avoid cities, too many people. She could go further north, but she'd probably face less work than she had now. She wanted more than anything to stay in Camden Cove. She mentally tallied up her tips from the tavern while deducting her splurge of coffee and a croissant, suddenly regretting spending the money. It wasn't enough to live off for long.

The older couple got up and left, leaving her all alone with her thoughts and worries. The man took his wife's hand as he opened the door and led her out of the bakery. She watched as he opened the car door for her, closing it once she got in.

She rested her head in her hand, thinking about all of her relationships with men. Even her own relationship with her father had ended after he left. Her mother never spoke of him. Never talked to Rachael or let her ask questions. He was just gone, and *they* had to get on.

As a kid, she had vowed not to end up like her mother, but she had ruined her chance at a normal life by falling for a guy like Nick. The worst part was that she had stayed even after she knew who he really was.

Even if Nick never found her, she'd never be able to live a normal life, she'd always be looking over her shoulder, hiding in the shadows. No, she'd never have the fairytale, the knight in shining armor, or the guy opening doors for her.

~

Jack sat at his desk when Frank walked in. "What's up?"

"Did you offer her a job?"

"What?"

"Rachael. Did you offer her a job?" his tone was sharp and scolding.

"Yes. Of course, I did. Why the interrogation?"

Frank made a face, sitting in the chair opposite Jack. "She was looking for some work this morning. I'm having her come in tomorrow."

"Doing what?" Jack couldn't imagine what they needed help with at this time of the year. The bakery had business, but nothing his uncles couldn't handle themselves.

"She's going to clean." Frank lifted his hands and shrugged. "Take stuff down, and other things. David's going to kill me. Your mother thinks I'm nuts."

Jack understood. His uncle had made up work for her. "That's really nice of you."

"Do you know her story?" Frank asked.

Jack shook his head, almost wondering if Frank did. He could get almost anyone to talk.

"I had to offer her something."

Frank got up from the chair and got serious again. "Offer her a job, again."

"I can try, but she's willing to work for everyone else in town, but me." He held up his hands in surrender. Why was he suddenly in the doghouse? "And hang out with old men."

Frank made a face.

If Frank only knew how hard he had tried, he'd understand

why Jack gave up. Over the past week, he had hardly seen her, except when she snuck around the restaurant so she wouldn't be seen.

"Old men?" Frank asked.

"She was with Finn the other night."

"Doesn't she work at the tavern?"

Jack started something he didn't want, which was to get other people involved. Especially his uncle, because that meant his mother would get involved, too.

"Oh, geez, I didn't notice the time. I have to…" Jack looked around for something he should be doing so he wouldn't have to answer the questions that were inevitably about to follow.

"Are you saying she went out with Finn McCabe?" Frank made a face. "He's old enough to be her grandfather."

"I think I hear my shipping order." Jack walked out of his office faster than Frank could get out of his chair and follow him.

"Did you see them together?" Frank asked after him, but Jack continued out the backdoor without answering.

Luckily, Frank didn't stick around. He left just as the dinner crowd started trickling in. As Jack managed the floor for the rest of the night, he thought about how to offer Rachael a job and have her actually accept it. He could almost guarantee that she would not agree to work for him, no matter how desperate her situation was. But that didn't mean he'd stop trying. Besides, Frank would continue to give him a hard time if he at least didn't offer again.

As he closed up the restaurant and headed out the back, he peeked up at the second floor. All the windows glowed out into the starry night. He glanced at the water as the waves crashed against the harbor. The bittersweet smell of autumn reminded him of the changes to come. He appreciated a fresh start, a new beginning, and he wanted more than anything to be able to provide that start for Rachael, if only she'd let him.

CHAPTER 7

*R*achael spent the morning on the trail, with the leash and collar in her coat pocket. Even though there was no sign of the dog, all the food she left the day before had been eaten. She filled the container with more kibble, hoping she wasn't feeding another critter.

The tide had gone out and the water seemed to reflect her mood. The waves glided onto the shore as the tiny sanderlings ran up and down. The horizon once again blended perfectly together with the sky. Only the whites of tumbling waves breaking onto the rocks could be seen and heard. She noticed that for the first time in a long time, she wasn't thinking about surviving. She hadn't been thinking much of anything besides looking for the dog... and maybe Jack.

She didn't even fool *herself* with the way she pretended not to look as she walked by his house, focusing her attention on the water. As though she hadn't noticed the house that she could almost see from the apartment. What was it about this guy? Her thoughts hadn't been stolen like this since... well... since Nick.

As she headed back home, when she passed Jack's place, she couldn't help herself, sneaking another glance, but his house looked empty. Jack was quite the workaholic. He spent most of his days and nights at the restaurant. Working long and hard was hardly a character flaw. She respected hard work.

As she reached the edge of his property, she noticed someone stood outside on the patio. Her heart fluttered unexpectedly, but when he turned, it wasn't Jack. She must've been staring, because he waved, walking toward her. The man must've thought he knew her.

She waved back instinctively but hurried along the trail as he walked closer.

"Hey, you're Rachael, right?"

She stopped and turned around. "Yes?"

"How do you like the apartment?" His smile seemed playful, and she could tell from the eyes that he meant no harm, but she didn't like the idea of this stranger knowing where she lived. "Excuse me?"

"Oh, sorry, I forgot you're new here." He stepped closer and reached out his hand. "I'm Matt, Jack's brother. Welcome to Camden Cove. Where everyone knows your business."

She slowly extended her hand, watching the side of his mouth quirk. "Hi."

"We met at the Tavern."

She should've been able to tell that he was related to Jack. They did have a lot of the same physical characteristics, including the eyes, green like a mid-summer pool.

"Nice to meet you." If Nick showed up, showing off his badge, asking about her, the whole town of Camden Cove would be able to tell him everything, apparently.

"I wanted to thank you for dumping that drink into Freddy's lap, that night."

She stopped, not really sure what to say, remembering where she knew Matt from. It really was a small town. She noticed the dark circles under his eyes. "You're welcome."

He gave her a look. "Jack can be a bit bossy, but his intentions are good."

"He told me about the bag of dog stuff."

"Oh." Why did she have to flip out? She had a feeling he wouldn't have said it if he knew she was technically still married, and running away from a monster.

"He means well, but he's like a puppy, still needs a lot of training." He gave her a smile. "I'm sure I'll see you around."

He headed back toward Jack's house. She hoped he wasn't going to go back to his wife who had done such a terrible thing to him. Not that it was any of her business. She of all people could never judge someone's relationship. But, she had learned, no matter how many promises someone made, they were only words. People don't change.

Jack stepped into the tavern, hoping to catch Rachael and keep his promise to his uncle, but only saw the regular waitresses and Finn.

"What can I get you?" Valerie asked. She had graduated the same year as him. She was already married with three kids. Would settling down ever be in the cards for him? Kids, and the whole nine yards? He saw the irony of being at the tavern, chasing after a girl who didn't seem to want to be around him. His uncle may have prompted him to go to the tavern, but he had happily complied.

He must be crazy.

"I was looking for the new girl. Is she working today?"

"No, not today, but Finn usually schedules her for nights."

"Jack, what are you doing here?" Finn said, walking out from the back.

"I was looking for Rachael." Jack looked around. Most of the tables had customers. "Business looks good."

"Leaf-peepers right now, but that's going to end soon." Finn shrugged.

Jack nodded, knowing the same fate lurked for his own restaurant.

"Hear about the storm?"

"No, when's that coming in?"

"Looks like a tropical storm coming up from the south." Finn pointed in the direction of the water. "They say in a few days. Flooding and power outages."

"Great." Jack mumbled something explicit under his breath. Storms along the coast were nothing to take lightly. Houses could and did get damaged every time one rolled in from the east. Would Rachael know what to do? Now he almost wished he hadn't pushed Rachael to move above the restaurant, out on the cove, alone.

The restaurant had always been a survivor, but even so, she shouldn't stay there. How would he convince her to leave?

As if his dad had read his mind, his phone rang. He didn't even get a chance to speak. "Hear about the storm?"

"Yup," Jack said. "Just heard from Finn."

"Want to stop by and grab the shutters, just in case?"

"Sure," Jack nodded. It was the last thing he wanted to do, but he was fooling himself with Rachael. She didn't need him telling her about a storm. She was very capable to take care of herself, he was learning.

"The sooner you get those shutters on, the sooner my heart can relax."

After he hung up with his dad, he said goodbye to Finn.

"Did you need to talk to Rachael?" Finn asked.

"Nah, I'll stop by another time." He headed out and swung by his parent's house. He and his dad pulled the shutters from the garage and then drove back to the restaurant. He planned to pop up to the apartment. He somehow convinced himself he should tell her about the storm. As he parked in his spot at the restaurant, he spotted her coming in off the trail.

"Hey." He waved at her. She waved back, which was a major improvement over ignoring his presence.

They met in the middle of the parking lot.

"Hey."

Jack shoved his hands into his pockets. "I just wanted to give you a heads-up about a storm coming in."

"I heard."

"I'm going to have to put up storm shutters on the windows."

"Will you need help?"

She shoved a black strap into her pocket, and he realized it was the leash he had given her. He almost smiled, but stayed neutral and shook his head.

He hesitated to ask, but then went for it. "Any luck?" He nodded toward the leash.

"No, nothing today. You?"

Jack shook his head. "Not since I saw him with you."

She nodded.

"Sorry again for not saying anything."

She shook her head. "It's okay."

"Are we good?"

Her eyes stayed on him this time. and she smiled. "Yeah, we're good."

"Are you sure you don't need a job?"

She made a face, but this time she hesitated, giving him hope. "Nope, I'm good."

Rachael listened as Frank told her about the big tropical storm coming up the coast.

"They're saying trees and power lines might come down with the high winds, and there's going to be flooding."

She stood on the ladder leaning against shelves along the bakery's brick wall. She passed down a wicker basket and passed it to Frank, who wiped it off with a wet towel.

"You obviously didn't need me." She realized this was a rescue mission, which was sweet and strange at the same time.

"It's a lot faster with two." Frank grabbed a gravy bowl and passed it to her. "I like having the extra hands, and I don't have to be the one on the ladder."

Her gut feeling made her think he was exaggerating. Frank had already climbed up on the ladder half a dozen times, rearranging the things on the shelves that she had cleaned and put back.

"So... where are you from?" Frank straightened a bread basket in the corner. It was friendly conversation, but friendly conversation or not, she didn't want to let her guard down.

"I'm from Rhode Island." She had rehearsed this for months, when she decided to leave Rachael Milano behind. Now she was Rachael Margaret Hawkins. Born in Boston, moved to Rhode Island as a kid. She'd left out the part about being married to Nicholas Milano, chief deputy of the Providence Police Department.

"I've never been." Frank had a very distinct accent. Maybe French? "But I've heard it's lovely."

"It's not like Maine, that's for sure." She climbed down the ladder and turned her back to him, hoping he'd stop with the questions.

The kitchen door swung open and out walked David, Frank's husband and the pastry chef. He carried a plate full of a golden something with steam rising up.

"Get down from there, Frank," he commanded. "Do you want to break your neck?"

Frank dangled from the ladder, arranging an old tea set. "I want to change things around a bit while Rachael does the dirty work."

David rolled his eyes and held the plate in front of Frank and Rachael. "I made tarte fines aux pommel. I'm thinking of making these for Mrs. Stevenson's retirement party. Try them and tell me if you like them."

Rachael assumed David was talking to Frank, so she returned to washing the shelves when he brought the plate closer to her.

"Come on, tell me what you think."

"Me?"

"Yes, I need opinions."

She wiped her hands on her jeans and took one of the pastries. David watched as she took a bite, waiting for her reaction. As soon as her tongue hit the flaky pastry, her mouth exploded with flavor, a sugary sweet apple filling inside a fluffy yet crisp pastry shell. It was one of the best things she had ever tasted.

"It's okay." Frank put the rest of his on the plate, wiping his fingertips on a dishcloth.

Rachael's eyes shot open. "It's better than okay, it's delicious. It's so flaky and moist, yet crispy and savory."

Frank shrugged. "It's not your best."

David handed the plate to her. "Please, Rachael, have the rest."

She grabbed another piece of pastry heaven and sat at the table next to her, stuffing it in her mouth. "It's so good."

David ignored Frank swinging from the top shelf and walked back to the kitchen. Rachael took another bite, savoring the sweet delicacy.

"He's so sensitive," Frank mumbled from above her. She couldn't help but smile. The two had been bickering all day in a quirky, sweet, and completely ridiculous sort of way. David continued to bring out pastries "to try" and Frank would ask for David's opinion about the new arrangements, even though "he didn't really care what he thought".

Usually, fighting couples made her anxiety run high. Anger mixed with hurt feelings never ended well in her household. Misunderstandings and pain happened, not desserts and sentiments. But every once in awhile, David complemented Frank's arrangements, and Frank bragged to Rachael about how talented a chef David was. It was clear they were crazy for each other.

By the end of the day, Frank had called it quits. "I'd love to have you return to finish up in here, and after that…" He looked around the room as if trying to think of something else Rachael could do. She didn't need to take any more of the kind men's time.

"I don't need to come back."

"No, this has been helpful, and I'd like you to finish." He hesitated, then asked, "Has my nephew offered you a job? You could really earn some good money at his place."

She shook her head. "I'd rather not."

"Really? He's great to work for."

She stayed quiet. How could she tell him that she didn't want to be a charity case, any more than she already was?

He raised his hands. "Okay, I won't push it."

She ignored the nagging feeling that she was lying to herself about the job. Jack never made her feel like a charity case. He made her feel something she hadn't felt in years, and she wasn't sure if she could trust herself with those kinds of feelings again.

It wasn't that she didn't trust him. She couldn't trust herself.

CHAPTER 8

*J*t hadn't been that long since Rachael arrived in Camden Cove, but already the small harbor town had started to feel like home. Her daily routine started with walking the trail, coming home and reading, then working at the tavern with Finn, and happy to start it all over the next day.

That morning, she found herself on the Coastal Trail looking back at the town harbor. She felt a strange sense of familiarity, as though she had lived there her whole life.

By now the locals seemed to recognize her, and some greeted her by name. Not to mention, half of them were Jack's family. Last night at the tavern, she had met his cousins. One even offered her a job on his boat, fishing, but she was pretty sure it was the alcohol talking and not an actual offer. Otherwise she'd take it, at this point. She'd take anything.

Well, almost anything.

Like always, she headed to the small inlet where she first saw the dog, carrying more food and water. Today, she planned to stay until she saw him again. With the storm coming, she didn't want to leave him all alone. Not that the blue sky overhead gave any warning. What was the old saying? The calm before the storm?

Was this her calm?

As she walked past Jack's house, she peeked only for a second before looking straight ahead. He hadn't been at the restaurant yet, but she knew he'd end up there. She could tell he was keeping his distance. She apparently gave off the crazy vibe well. She almost felt bad that he had been so nice to her. There was nowhere to go with her. Which was a shame, because the longer she stuck around, the more she realized he might be one of the good ones. Who was she kidding? He *was* one of the good ones.

The seagulls called out above her, as she climbed down to the sandy groove inlet. Sea grass sprung out from between the rocks, and there was a soft smell of beach, toasted sand baked by the sun. The tide had been out long enough to see the footprints of seagulls and clam holes, but nothing else.

She walked down the beach, watching the birds fly in the wind, when she noticed a different set of footprints. Dog footprints. People walked their dogs a lot on the trail, but this set of prints didn't have human prints shadowing them. If they were the dog's, he had to be close.

The footsteps ran along the seam where rocks met beach, zigzagging in and out and around the shore, sometimes disappearing into the water to return to the wet sand. After fifty yards, they disappeared up a small path leading back to the main trail. The gravel path showed no individual footprints, but she followed it.

As she reached the top of the bluff, where the trail connected, she caught sight of him – or he let her see him. By the way he watched her, she knew he was in charge.

"Hi, Captain." The name seemed perfect. She crouched down, slowly extending her hand toward him. "I was just looking for you."

The dog stood, cocking his head to the side as she spoke. He didn't move away from her, but instead sat. Waiting.

"Are you hungry?" She opened her bag, pulling out the food.

He cocked his head to the other side and stayed where he was.

When she pulled out the container, he stood up and his tail began to wag.

"That's it." He came a bit closer, apprehensive. She set the food next to her feet. "Come on, boy."

Captain tiptoed two feet ahead, then one step back, uneasy. When he was about a foot away, he lost all his inhibition and went right to the food, scarfing everything down. He licked the container, then Rachael's hand.

Tears sprung to her eyes as she laughed at his wet tongue against her skin. "That's a good boy, you must've been hungry."

She scratched behind his ears and his whole body leaned into it. Most of his fur was wet and matted down. He leaned harder against her one hand as she reached for the collar and leash inside her sweatshirt's pocket. "Okay, Captain, we're going to get you some help."

As soon as she pulled her hand away from his neck and inched the collar around, he took off.

She began making kissing noises and whistles. "Come back, Captain, come!"

He continued to run and she took off after him, determined not to let him get away this time. He ran further ahead, faster, and before she knew it, he was gone.

As Jack turned down Harbor Lane, he noticed activity outside his uncle's bakery, but couldn't make out what was happening until he parked his truck alongside the road. A small crowd gathered behind a delivery van. Rachael and David knelt, huddled together. The door to the shop was wide open. Frank was with them, but talking on the phone. What were they all leaning over?

When he got closer, he made out the figure lying on the ground. The dog. "Oh, no."

Jack ran over, crouching down next to Rachael and his uncles on the ground. Rachael held the dog's head in her lap. There was blood under his hind leg. The dog whined, trying to stand up on his front legs, but unable to. David leaned over him, holding him down. Jack could see a large laceration.

The dog tried to get up again but fell back. His whining became more panicked.

Rachael talked in a calm voice. "It's going to be okay, Captain." She stroked the dog's head slowly, over and over, shushing him. "We're going to take care of you."

"What happened?"

"I ran after him." Rachael looked up at him. Tears swelled in her eyes. "I shouldn't have run after him, otherwise he wouldn't have gone out into the road."

"Elizabeth said to wrap his leg up to stop the bleeding," Frank stuffed his phone in his pocket. "To tie it tight and apply pressure."

Jack pulled off his button-up leaving him in an undershirt. He ripped the sleeve off and wrapped the dog's leg. He whined, but didn't move much in Rachael's hands. Thank God for his sister Elizabeth.

"We don't want to move the leg too much," Frank said.

"I didn't see the dog in the mirror until it was too late." The driver of the truck was visibly shaken up.

"Let's get him to the clinic," Frank said.

"I'll grab my truck." Jack ran off to where he had parked, jumped in, and barreled back.

"I'm going with you." Rachael kept her focus on the dog, but he could see her alarm.

Jack nodded and swept the animal into his arms. "You hold him while I drive."

She didn't say anything, just nodded. He almost commented on the fact that she didn't argue with him but didn't want to waste any time. They needed to get the dog to his sister's clinic as soon as possible. In his arms, the dog felt like skin and bones. He clearly hadn't had a regular meal in a long time.

"I'll get the door." Frank ran in front of them. Rachael jumped in the passenger's seat and Jack placed the dog in her lap.

He jumped in the truck, then floored it to the clinic, hoping the dog would hang on. Elizabeth would know what to do.

"How far is the vet?" She made shushing noises to the dog as it whimpered in her arms.

"It's right up here, not even a mile." Jack pointed up the road. "My sister Elizabeth will take care of him."

"Your sister's the vet? Are you related to everyone in town?"

Jack looked at her and smiled. "Basically."

Soon, they saw the sign for the clinic. He was relieved when he saw that only a couple of cars were parked in the lot.

Jack helped Rachael out of the truck as Elizabeth opened the front door once they got up the steps.

"Dr. Johnson's already in the examination room." Elizabeth led them down the hall and into the room. "Get him on the table, and I'll give him a sedative to calm him down."

The dog whined as Jack laid him down, but didn't move. He panted heavily as Elizabeth examined him.

"It looks like he's just cut, no broken bones that I can see, but I'm worried he might have internal injuries," Elizabeth said. "We'll take some x-rays and check everything out."

"I'll pay," Rachael said. Everyone looked at her. "For the x-rays. I can pay."

"No, I'll pay." Jack pulled out his wallet.

"No, I will."

"Don't you need to ask your landlord if you're allowed dogs?"

She huffed, crossing her arms against her chest as the door opened, and David and Frank rushed into the room.

"How's he doing?" Frank said.

David walked straight to Elizabeth. "Will he be okay?"

"Where should I pay?" Jack asked.

Elizabeth held up her hands to the group. "Look, you all have to go to the waiting room, and you can figure the money stuff out there." Even as a little kid, she always bossed the older boys around. "I'll call when he's in recovery."

"I'll leave my number at the front desk," Rachael said. "I can take him home."

Jack stepped back, looking at her. "*I* can take him home."

"Seriously?" Rachael's mouth dropped open. "*You* want Captain?"

Elizabeth, Frank, and David all looked at him.

"You named him?"

"Doesn't he deserve a name?"

"Yes, I guess so." He hadn't really thought about taking the dog, now named Captain, but how was she going to afford a dog? And an injured one? "I could use some company. Plus, I have a house and a yard."

He almost said *and the money*, but stopped himself just in time.

"Alright, we need to get whoever's dog into x-rays." Elizabeth pushed all four of them out into the lobby. As Rachael and his uncles filed out, Elizabeth grabbed Jack's arm and pulled him back to the examination room, closing the door behind them.

"Really, Jack?" Elizabeth made a face at him. "The dog's going to need a lot of extra care for the next few weeks, at least. Plus, he's going to have to come back and get check-ups to see if he's healing alright. You can hardly take care of your houseplants."

"I'm going to have extra time, now that winter's coming."

"You're definitely going to need time."

She eyed him, still holding onto his arm.

"What?"

"Did you ever think she doesn't want your help?"

"Yes."

"Then why are you being so persistent, here?"

Jack let out a deep sigh. "Because she might change her mind."

~

Rachael sat in the small apartment, holding her phone. Jack's sister had promised to call as soon as Captain was taken care of. Even though she didn't have the money, or had technically asked her landlord if she could have a dog, she wasn't giving in. She wanted Captain.

She couldn't believe Jack was fighting for him. Actually, she could believe it. The guy loved to nosedive in. He reminded her of a cartoon superhero. But she didn't need him.

She got up from the couch, her eyes immediately on the water. The gray waves and sky seemed endless. Now, it looked like a storm was approaching.

Jack was most likely downstairs in the kitchen. He may have been right about everything he said at the veterinarian clinic. He had the house and yard, and the wherewithal to take good care of the dog, but she *needed* Captain.

She grabbed her keys off the counter. Leaving the lights on, she left and ran down the stairs. The screen door slapped shut as she walked into the kitchen. The afternoon shift had only one cook behind the counter, and a couple waitresses stood in the kitchen. Even his popular restaurant's business had begun to fizzle out. Which proved everything she had thought. He was offering her a job as charity, and she was no charity case.

"I want the dog." She spoke as soon as he walked into the kitchen.

"Fine." He didn't even really look at her, just walked by her into the office.

She opened her mouth to argue, but then realized he had agreed. "Fine?"

"If you want him that bad, take him." Jack gave her a look, then shut his door.

She stood there, frozen, thinking of her next move, rubbing her thumb. She had a whole argument planned out in her head. He wasn't supposed to give in that easily. In fact, she wasn't going to let him give in that easily. She grabbed the door knob and burst through the door.

"And I'm not your charity case, either." She hooked one hand on her hip as she pointed a finger at him. He settled in behind the desk, keeping his eyes on her. "If you don't allow dogs, then I'll find some place that does."

"Fine."

"Fine, I can have a dog? Or fine, I should find another place?"

"Fine, you can have him." He leaned back in his chair. "Only if I get to pay for his medical bills."

There it was. "No."

"Why is my help so horrible to accept?"

She fisted both hands on her hips. "Because I don't need it. I'm perfectly fine taking care of myself."

"I know."

"Then why don't you stop trying to pretend what you're doing isn't just some sort of charity?"

"If that's what you think I'm doing."

It *was* what she thought he was trying to do. "I mean, I just want to help the dog."

"So did I." His shoulders slumped, his expression changing. He looked defeated, and a strange guilt flooded over her, as though she had been the one crossing the line. She squeezed her fingers. "I mean, I know you think you're helping me, but I'm fine."

"Let me know if you need anything for him, though. I'm sure my sister will help you out."

"I'm okay." Rachael suddenly felt childish and embarrassed by her rant. "I just don't need help."

"You said." He looked over at his computer screen, facing away from her.

"You're better off, believe me, not associating with me." She kept talking for some reason she didn't understand, strangely incapable of stopping. "Because I'm like that storm coming in. I'm unpredictable."

He looked back at her, looked deep into her eyes. "It's all in your perspective, I guess."

"What do you mean?"

He leaned over his desk, closer to where she stood. "You see a storm, and I see energy and strength."

"You don't need a waitress," she snapped back at him.

He shook his head. "Nope."

"And I can pay for Captain's medical bills myself."

"Stop." He held up his hands.

"Just because I don't have a restaurant on the water—"

"No, it's not that." He held up his phone. "It's my sister."

He answered, but didn't talk at first, driving Rachael mad with anxiety.

"Is he okay?" She leaned closer to his desk, trying to hear what his sister was saying on the other end. Her heart pounded in her ears, which made her unable to hear.

"How long?" he asked. "Will he be okay?"

He covered the phone with his hand and said, "His leg is sprained, and he got stitches. She wants him to stay at least the night to keep an eye on him." He hesitated. "Are you sure you want this dog?"

"Yes." She did. She wanted Captain more than she had wanted anything in her life. Something in her needed to help him. "Will you be okay with that?"

"With the way you two were together on the beach, you deserve him."

Rachael couldn't contain her smile, so she covered it with her hands.

"But only if I pay for the medical bills."

She dropped her arms. Her lips pressed together, emotions flooding her eyes.

"Whether you wanted the dog or not, I would've paid." Jack shook his head. "Just let me pay."

"You really don't know how to stop." She let out a breath, but it felt like more like a sigh of relief.

"Nope."

CHAPTER 9

*R*achael ran over to the veterinarian clinic on her lunch break. Finn had wrapped a sandwich for her, over her protests. She was grateful, even though she couldn't, for some reason, allow herself to show it.

The cheerful assistant behind the counter greeted her right away. "You're back."

Rachael nodded. "Is it okay if I see him again?"

"Rachael!" Dr. Elizabeth stepped into the lobby from the back room. "I thought I'd see you soon. He's been sleeping, mostly, but he's still really skittish around us. You seem to have a way with him, though."

Elizabeth walked her back to the kennels where Captain lay. He and another dog were the only two in the room. When he saw her, he lifted his head and his tail wagged a bit. He stumbled to get up on his front legs. Elizabeth smiled. "He does seem to know you."

"Can I go in?"

"Yes, of course."

Rachael held out her hands, shushing Captain as he whimpered and struggled. His tail smacking against the floor. "Sit down, little man, before you hurt yourself."

She sat close to him on the floor. He stretched his head out, letting her scratch behind his ears, and soon rested it in her lap.

"Who's been a good boy?"

His tail flopped as he pushed his head against her hand.

"He's such a phony." Elizabeth laughed. "He acted like the world had come to an end when you were away."

Rachael smiled at Captain's big brown eyes looking up at her. She liked him, too. "No cone of shame anymore?"

"We took the cone off, since he seems to be leaving his wound alone." Elizabeth rubbed his head. "He could probably head home as soon as tomorrow, but he's not going to be able to climb up and down those stairs of yours," Elizabeth said. "I think he should stay here since you're on the second floor."

Rachael's heart dropped. She didn't want him there any longer than he needed to be. Not that they weren't taking good care of him, but she wanted to be with him. Not to mention the fact that she wouldn't be able to afford it. "I can carry him up and down."

"He needs to be crated. Plus, now that he has a steady diet, he's going to start gaining weight. He's going to be heavy."

Rachael wasn't a pixie, she could certainly carry him up and down a flight of steps. "I'll be okay."

"You have no yard, which means you'd have to carry him somewhere." Elizabeth's voice sounded soft. "I know this is not what you want to hear, but let me take him until he gets better."

Rachael started to interrupt her, but Elizabeth spoke before she could.

"You can stay with us, too," Elizabeth said quickly.

"Are you serious?" Rachael couldn't believe this family. What else could they do for her? "I couldn't."

"Seriously, you should, with the storm coming. You shouldn't be in that apartment hanging over the water during the blow."

Rachael hadn't really thought about leaving because of the storm. Finn had offered earlier, she could stay with him, but he probably didn't want a stray dog.

Elizabeth continued, "Captain will need at least a few days to get back to walking normally, and you can't lug him up and down the stairs in a tropical storm." She shook her head. "Just stay at my place. We have plenty of room, and people to look after him."

Rachael didn't want him to be alone again.

"You're smack dab in the middle of the water, out there." Elizabeth shook her head. "You and Captain can stay with me and my family, at least until the storm is over."

Rachael wanted to argue, but how could she, with Captain's face looking up at her like that? She didn't want to put him in danger, or herself. She'd pay for the nights she stayed, buy food, and even cook for Elizabeth. She'd clean and do whatever she needed to repay her for everything. Rachael needed to start repaying her debts.

～

"They said four to five inches of flooding." David leaned on his shovel as he relayed the facts to Jack.

All of the Williams men stood outside in the parking lot. Earlier that day, Matt and his friend Dan had dumped a pile of sand. Jack had pulled out the familiar sandbags from storms past. Everyone had brought shovels and tools to help protect the buildings from the storm rumbling up the coast.

"We should've had the football team come down here and volunteer," John said.

Jack handed out bags to all the men. "That's not a bad idea."

They all looked at the pile of sand, a long day's work in front of them. Off in the distance, he saw Rachael walking up Harbor Lane. He wondered how Captain was recuperating. He had to admit he liked the name.

She stopped at the sand pile and asked, "Can I help?"

Jack leaned against his shovel. "We're good."

She shot him a look, instantly ready to fight. "I can help."

"You could hold open the bags," Matt said, struggling to dump his load of sand.

She narrowed her eyes at Jack, walking toward Matt's sand spilling over the bag's edges. She leaned down and held it open, turning her back to Jack.

Why was he such an idiot, sometimes? He shook his head as he filled the rest of his sandbag. He was hopeless when it came to this woman.

After a couple of hours, the pile had been bagged and the bags had been stacked in front of the building's doors and weak spots. Other business owners also sandbagged the front of their businesses. Frank pulled through and actually found high-schoolers to come down to volunteer. The girls' soccer team had the biggest turnout.

Before he knew it, most of the community had come down, including the rest of his family. Jack had his cooks make fish chowder and fresh rolls for the group of volunteers. All the while, Rachael stayed and helped. She held open the bags, and shoveled her own. She carried the sandbags across the road, piling them in front of the storefronts and around the buildings. She never once complained or slowed down, even when Jack felt like it.

At the end of the day, when the sky faded into a silky navy blue with a few stars winking through the clouds, he snuck a glance at her. Even after all that work, she still looked beautiful.

Rachael picked up a shovel that leaned against a parking meter and handed it over to him.

"Thanks," he said.

"No, I'm the one who owes you a thank-you." He could see her breath as she spoke. "I haven't been fair to you, and I'm sorry."

The apology took him by surprise and his body suddenly radiated with heat, even standing in the cool night. He was drawn to her like steel to a magnet. He couldn't keep his eyes off her.

"You don't have to be sorry." He had a harder time accepting her apology than she did giving it. "I can be a bit persistent at times."

She gave him a look.

"Okay," he laughed. "A lot persistent, but I mean well."

She nodded. "That I believe is true."

She didn't say anything else, just stood there. He didn't want to ask, but he couldn't help but worry. "You should think about staying somewhere other than the apartment when the storm hits. I have an extra room, if you need it."

"Your sister's letting me and Captain stay with her."

Of course, Elizabeth would think of that. "That's perfect."

She looked at her watch. "I should probably head to the tavern before the town wants their last drink before the storm." She walked backwards as she spoke.

Jack held up the shovel. "I should probably clean up the rest of this stuff."

She nodded, looking as though she wanted to say something else, hesitating. "You should stop by."

He almost dropped the shovel to the ground. "Sure," he said, before she could change her mind.

"I'll see you then."

He didn't move until she was gone. Then, he swept everything up and closed up the restaurant in no time, rushing back to his place to wash up. But when he walked into the house, all the lights were out, even though Matt's truck was in the driveway.

"Matt?" He dropped his keys on the counter, opening up the fridge to look for a snack before heading to the tavern. When he turned on the light, Matt startled him, sitting at the table.

"Hey," Matt mumbled.

"Want to go to the tavern?" Jack looked up from the fridge.

Matt pushed a set of papers across the table toward Jack. "Looks like she wants a divorce."

"Ah, man, I'm sorry." Jack shook his head and sat down at the table, looking at the papers, the decree formal and fitting for Justine.

"Are you?"

Jack leafed through the papers. Irreconcilable differences had been checked off. "I'm sorry you're going through this."

Matt nodded, but didn't look up. He fiddled with a loose string hanging from his shirt. "I think I'm going to stay in tonight."

"Want to talk about it?"

Matt made a face. "No."

Jack threw the papers back down on the table. "Want to help put the storm shutters up on the house?"

Matt sighed. "Since it looks like I'm stuck here, I should probably earn my keep."

Jack rolled his eyes, but he knew Matt would be okay. It'd take time, he knew how long it could take to heal from this kind of hurt, but Matt would come around.

He got up and headed to his truck to grab his toolbox. "We can start upstairs."

Matt nodded, getting up from the table, folding up the documents sitting in front of him. "I'll grab a couple beers."

Rachael wasn't looking for him, she told herself over and over as she stood behind the counter with Finn. But every time the door opened and the bell jingled against the glass, she'd look to see if it was Jack. By the end of the night, after most of the regulars had left, her hopes had faded. What had gotten into her that afternoon? She wasn't even sure why she had asked him to come. She knew how dangerous it was to get close to someone. What if he found out she wasn't technically Rachael Hawkins?

It was better that Jack hadn't shown up. The only thing Rachael had was Rachael, and she had even lost herself along the way.

No more.

Jack might be a great guy, from a great family, but he was

better off without her, and she was better off without him. And just as she reminded herself how very wrong Jack Williams was for the last time, the bell jingled. Her eyes immediately went to the front of the tavern. There, framed in the doorway, stood Jack.

Her stomach did a little loop-de-loop.

She looked down at the tray of drinks. She had forgotten what she had been doing before he walked in. She stared at the empty glasses and then looked up again. This time she caught his eye, and just as quickly darted her eyes away. Holy moly, he looked good. Her face warmed at the thought. There was no mistaking the look he was giving her.

She took in a deep breath and picked up the tray, remembering she had been bringing them to the kitchen. As she walked back behind the bar, she kept the Williams brothers in her peripheral vision, just enough to see where they sat, but not enough to make him think she was looking. Jack, however, didn't mind looking. His gaze settled on Rachael and she could feel him looking at her even with her back facing him. When she turned, he nodded and smiled, but she shot her eyes in a different direction.

Smooth, she thought to herself, as she poured more drinks. She filled the tray and brought it out to one of her tables. She passed the drinks around and offered to get anything else, for anyone, anything to stall before having to face Jack.

Then she felt a tap on her shoulder.

"Hey." He stood behind her, his hands stuffed in his jeans pockets. His face was pink from being out in the cold. His eyebrow lifted. A bit of mischief flickered across his face as he stood waiting for her to respond.

"Hey." *Classy*. She wanted to smack her forehead.

"So... how's your night?" He rolled a bit back on his heels.

"Good, busy."

The place had been filled with regulars.

"The storm." Jack looked around. "Last night for Finn's brew."

"We've never been busier." She laughed, thinking about how on a Sunday night, the place was mobbed.

"No one has anywhere to go, once it hits." He stepped closer, and she could smell his musky scent. "Are you working the whole night?"

She looked at the clock. It was just past nine. "Until closing."

He had that look again. Just as he was about say something else, the bell rang against the door, catching his attention. "You've got to be kidding me."

Rachael turned to see Freddy walking inside.

From the corner of her eye, she saw Matt push his stool back and stand, like a wolf ready to strike its prey.

Freddy made no secret that he saw Matt, too. He gave his buddy a pat on the stomach and the two of them laughed as they walked to a table across the room. "We're here to celebrate!"

"Oh, no."

Matt charged across the room toward Freddy. Jack thrust his drink into her hand and ran toward the commotion. Freddy almost didn't seem to care that Matt, now a speeding bull, raged toward his table. Matt didn't slow down as he reached Freddy. His arm swung back before Jack could grab it, and he punched Freddy square in the jaw. Freddy stumbled back, his hands grabbing for his face. All of Freddy's friends jumped up out of their seats and pounced Matt, just as Jack dove between them.

Rachael froze. Her knees locked, and she couldn't move from where she stood. She had been around plenty of fights in the past. So, this shouldn't have been a thing, but her heart raced. She shook in place as she watched the men yelling and pushing each other. Her breath got stuck inside her chest as others moved around her, bumping into her. The whole room felt unsteady. Jack's glass slipped out of her hand and fell to the floor almost in slow motion, smashing against the wood, spraying every surrounding surface.

She didn't look back as she left the floor. Walking past Finn, she said, "I'm taking ten." But she didn't even wait for him to say anything before she left out the back door.

The cool night air hit her as she stepped outside. She shook out her hands as she walked in a circle in the back alley by the garbage dumpster. Her heart pounded in her ears. She understood Matt's reaction. His anger had nothing to do with her. Why was she freaking out this way?

If she concentrated hard enough, she could hear the pounding rhythm of the waves against the coast. She squeezed her eyes shut, trying to focus on the water, pacing.

She didn't know how long she had been outside, when Jack stepped out. "Hey, you okay?"

"Yeah, I'm fine." She held her arms against her chest, not sure what to say. "I just needed some air."

He nodded, but his eyebrows creased together. "Freddy's gone, you can go back inside."

She let out a deep breath and nodded, but she could feel her heart racing still.

"Everyone should be cooled down by now," Jack said, almost as though he read her mind. "I'm taking Matt home."

"Oh." Her chest was still tight.

"Do you want me to come back and bring you home after closing?"

She shook her head. "No, but thanks. I'll be okay."

He stuffed his hands in his pockets and then smiled. "I know you'll be okay. I'd just like to. There's a difference."

She knew he was only being nice. The sensible thing would be to say yes, since she really didn't want to walk home alone.

"Thanks, but I'm good."

He smiled again but shook his head. "At least ask Finn to drive you home, okay?"

She watched him walk back inside, finally taking in a deep breath of the cold air.

After closing, she ended up asking Finn to drop her off. She checked around the apartment. All the lights were left on, even in the closet. Nothing had been moved around. Everything was folded and in the same place, just the way she left it that morning.

Nothing was wrong. Nick wasn't coming. She kept telling herself that.

She had nothing to worry about.

Nothing.

CHAPTER 10

*J*ack didn't feel right about snooping, but something told him that Rachael was in trouble. A kind of trouble that she couldn't handle on her own. That woman's pride was bigger than his, which was saying something. He should have just ignored what his instincts were telling him, but there he was, standing in Camden Cove's police station, pretending to be "stopping by" to visit his buddy Alex.

"What are you doing here?" Alex said, surprised to see him.

Jack shrugged before giving him a combination handshake and bro hug. "I was in the area and wondered if you could do me a favor."

His friend narrowed his eyes. "What are you up to, Williams?"

Jack made sure no one else was listening. "I was wondering if you could tell me anything about the woman who's renting the apartment above the restaurant."

Alex's left eyebrow lifted. "You mean the very attractive woman who just came to town?"

"Who I think is in trouble."

"You do know that's what the internet is for these days." Alex patted Jack on the back. "Ask Alexa."

"Yes, but then why have a best friend who's a police officer?"

Alex shook his head. "Why do I do the things I do for you and your brother?"

"My brother?"

Alex rubbed his chin. "Freddy wanted to press charges last night."

Jack could feel his blood pressure start to rise. "Freddy wants to press charges?"

"Don't worry, I calmed him down." Alex walked through the station to his office. "Lucky, too, because your brother's right hook did some good damage to his face."

"The knuckle punch." Their father had taught them that move as kids.

"Wish I could've seen it." Alex smiled as they walked into his office.

"It was quite a sight." Jack shut the door behind them. "So, can you help me?"

"I might, but…"

"What?"

Alex shrugged. "I always find when someone isn't willing to talk about their past, it's usually because they're hiding something." He let out a deep breath and tapped his pen against his desk. "I'll get to it, if I get to it. This isn't really what my job is about."

"Thanks, man. I just want to make sure she's going to be okay."

When Jack left Alex's office, the sky above him swirled as the storm rolled into town. Whitecaps foamed at the top of the waves. He didn't bother going to the restaurant. No need, since none of his workers could even make it in to work. Nor would there be anyone willing to eat out. Even Finn closed the tavern, and he barely closed on a holy day.

He turned the television on as soon as he got home.

"There's going to be a lot of precipitation with this storm," the meteorologist said to the screen. "Expect major flooding conditions. Don't drive through any moving water. There could be flash flooding, and you do not want to get swept up without warning."

Jack felt like a prisoner in his own house with all the storm shutters on, covering up any light that penetrated the clouds. The rain had already started, blowing in from the water, smacking against the house. They'd lose power most likely. He worried most about the wind doing damage.

As the daylight faded and the rain fell even harder, he decided he'd be better off at his parents' house. Matt had already packed up and headed over. Maybe he should hit up his sister's place, stop in to check on how they were doing. It wouldn't hurt to make sure everyone was alright.

When he arrived, however, Elizabeth had no shame when she answered the door.

"Look who's here!" The wide smile plastered on her face, along with her loud announcement of his presence, made everyone stop what they were doing and look at him. He should've known Elizabeth would see through his kindness.

Rachael was in mid-step, carrying a bowl of spaghetti from the kitchen. He felt like a teenager who had a girl over at the house, which he tried not to do because of exactly what Elizabeth was doing.

"Did you know that Rachael can cook really good Italian food?" Elizabeth said. Then, covering the side of her mouth with her hand, she said, "Like mom."

She winked at Jack before turning to Rachael. He rolled his eyes, but his jaw dropped as she stood there, holding the heaping bowl of pasta. He felt a serious Freudian complex as the room heated up as he looked at her in an apron.

Rumbling down the back staircase, Lucy, Elizabeth's step-daughter, ran up to him and gave him a hug. "Uncle Jack, did you meet Rachael?"

"Yes, I have."

Elizabeth laughed. "Would you like to join us for dinner, Romeo?"

"Um… only if that's okay with everybody?" he asked, but looked only at Rachael.

She placed the bowl on the table and her hands on her hips. He waited for her to say no. "That sounds great."

Was Rachael finally warming up to him? Or just learning to deal with him?

Adam walked over and gave Jack a handshake. "Want something to drink?"

"Nah, man, I'm good." Jack looked for the dog. "Where's Captain?"

Rachael nodded toward the wood stove on the other side of the kitchen. Captain was sprawled out, lying between Elizabeth's other two dogs, as though it had been his spot forever.

"He looks right at home." He walked over to the dog, whose tail wagged as he approached him. "How's he doing?"

Lucy crouched down beside him, scratching her little fingers on Captain's forehead. "He's doing great, but he's trying to walk around on his leg."

"I gave him a little something to calm him down." Elizabeth walked over with a beer in her hand and passed it over to him. "He took to the farm, let's just say."

Elizabeth and Adam's eighteenth-century colonial sat on over thirty acres of pastures and woods filled with trails. A dream for any dog.

Jack held up his hand to Elizabeth. "No, thanks, I'm headed to mom and dad's afterwards. I just wanted to check in to see if you needed anything."

Elizabeth gave it to him anyways. "Sit down."

"Join us," Rachael said from across the room.

Jack almost fell over as Rachael said it, but got up and followed Lucy to the table. He decided to change the subject. "I can't believe you got another person to cook for you," he teased his sister. Elizabeth had somehow gone through life without ever having to cook a meal for herself.

"Ha, ha." Elizabeth said, sitting in her chair. "Rachael kindly offered."

"I was happy to cook." Rachael picked up the bread basket and handed it over to Elizabeth.

"Rachael, relax," Elizabeth said.

She looked down at her hands, holding the basket. "Oh, sorry." She set the basket down.

Adam set a bowl of grated cheese in the middle of the table, then said, "Let's eat!"

Elizabeth smiled and held up her water glass. "To Captain."

Adam raised his own, while Lucy used her chocolate milk. Jack held up his beer to Rachael's wine glass. "To Captain."

She wished she hadn't thought about what it would be like to kiss him after her glass of wine. Now, as he sat in front of her with the power out and all of Elizabeth's candles lit, it was all she could think about. How very luscious his lips looked.

"I should probably head to Mom and Dad's." He got up from the kitchen table. They had been talking for a couple of hours, through dinner and dessert. Elizabeth poured Rachael another glass of wine.

"You can stay on the couch." Elizabeth held out another beer from the fridge. "It's not safe to drive out there."

A wave of disappointment washed over Rachael as he shook his head. She didn't want him to leave. She was enjoying herself with him there, with Captain and Elizabeth's family. Lucy had shown her the barn and all the animals as Adam and Jack checked on the Red Sox. Now they all sat at the table again around with the wood stove glowing in the background.

"Yes, stay," she said. Both Jack and Elizabeth stopped and looked at her.

"She's right. Stay!" Lucy jumped up. "It's like a big sleepover!"

Jack looked from Elizabeth to Rachael to Adam, who shrugged. "Fine, I'll stay on the couch."

"Good, you can help with Captain. He'll need to go out soon." Elizabeth stood up and walked into the kitchen, yawning.

A buzz floated inside Rachael's body. She enjoyed every part of the night. She loved listening to Camden Cove stories and legends from the sea. She even joined in razzing Jack with Elizabeth. Mostly, she liked how he kept looking at her with that smile, and how safe she felt, sitting across from him. Captain even took to Jack, crawling under the table to lie across his feet.

The night had been perfect.

It was Elizabeth who announced going to bed. "Well, I better get some rest. There's sure to be someone who'll need help with an animal."

Adam walked over to Lucy, who lay with the dogs on the floor, reading a book. "It's time for bed, little lady."

"Just one more chapter?" she pleaded.

Adam shook his head. "You may not have school tomorrow, but you have plenty of chores. Let's go." He picked up the blanket that covered her, and she stood without looking up from the book.

Lucy muttered something under her breath as she got up from the floor. She kissed all three dogs and pounded toward the table.

"Say goodnight to everyone," Elizabeth instructed her daughter.

"Good night." Jack held out his arms and she hugged him.

"Night, Uncle Jack." She squeezed his stomach.

He pretended she had hurt him, and groaned. "Sleep well."

Lucy ran up the stairs with Adam behind her

Elizabeth walked around, picking up a few things from the table.

"I'll clean up." Rachael stood up, clearing the glasses off the table.

"Thanks." Elizabeth yawned again. "I'm going to help with bedtime."

"Go, we can clean up." Jack picked up some leftover napkins and glasses and followed Rachael into the kitchen.

"Joan!" Elizabeth called for her cat from the staircase. She'd been hiding since Captain came inside the house.

Rachael set the glasses in the dishwasher, then faced him. "Well, good night, Jack." She sounded more formal than she meant to.

"Stay up with me." He pointed to the clock. "I mean, it's not even nine o'clock. Do you play cards?"

"Like... Go Fish?" When was the last time she had?

He made a face and laughed a little. "Well, if that's all you know. But I was thinking more like five-card draw, or gin rummy?"

"I know how to play cards." She rolled her eyes at him, suddenly feeling extra comfortable. She followed him into the living room and sat down on the couch as he opened a cabinet. Inside, there were all different types of board games stacked on top of each other. Through a small crevice, he pulled out a worn deck of cards.

"She stole these from my parents!" His mouth opened wide, as though he was upset. "I can't believe she was the one."

Jack sat on the floor next to the coffee table and shuffled the deck, gliding the cards into a bridge and tossing them like a dealer. "Rummy?"

"Seven cards." Rachael began to sort her hand. She raised her eyebrow as high as Jack's, as they each examined the cards.

"So you know more than go fish?" he teased, lining the deck.

"My grandfather liked to have friendly games together." For a second she almost told him about Finn, told him about their relationship, but was interrupted when he threw down three fives.

"Bam!"

She smiled behind her cards, but kept a poker face as she drew a card from the pile. Then she threw down a run from nine to queen. Then she discarded. He picked up a card, but kept his eyes on her. The game didn't last more than five rounds, with Rachael putting down the rest of the run along with three aces.

Jack watched as she shuffled the deck.

"What?" she laughed.

"You're good at cards."

She shrugged. "A little."

Nick had admired her skill in playing cards. When they first got married, they had game night once a month with his friends. He loved the way she gathered the cards together, shuffling and sorting, and tossing the cards out to the players. He'd brag to his friends about how well she played.

She shook the thoughts of Nick away and directed her attention back to Jack. "Does your family always get along so well?"

"Not when we all lived under one roof, but yes, for the most part, we get along."

She nodded as she dealt out the cards.

"How about you?" he asked. "You come from a big family?"

She shook her head. "No, just me and my mom, really."

She thought about Finn, probably sitting in his recliner, watching the news. Then she thought about her mom. Should she call her? Nick would have gone to her place by now.

"Finn tells me you're from Rhode Island."

"I lived outside of Providence, in a little town called Scituate."

"That's a nice city, Providence. I went to school at Johnson and Wales. My roommate was from Cranston."

"You're kidding?" She couldn't believe Jack had practically lived down the road. "I waited tables at Piccadilly's."

"I know that place." Jack smiled again, which made every part of her body tingle. "I definitely spent a couple evenings there."

"What made you come to Camden Cove?" he asked, as she sorted out his cards.

She didn't answer, instead pretending to arrange her hand. It was such a simple question, but involved so many complicated answers. If she was honest, she liked Jack. A lot. He was a gentleman who really did seem genuine, like the kind of guy she'd be proud to bring home, especially to Finn. But she couldn't tell him the truth.

"I stayed here as a kid and never forgot about it." She looked into the candle flames, and thought about herself as a little girl, running on the beach. "It just seemed like the perfect place to go for a fresh start."

"I'm glad you came."

She could see his expression change. He examined her as though he was studying a map, trying to navigate where to go next, and that's when she suddenly realized that she wasn't worried he'd hurt her, she was worried that she'd hurt him.

Jack lay on the couch looking up at the ceiling, listening as the wind and rain whipped against the windows. It sounded as though someone threw buckets of water at the glass. Luckily, the storm hadn't been as bad as they predicted, but he couldn't say the same about his feelings.

They were out of control.

He didn't necessarily mean to push her into talking, but he knew he had stepped over a very delicate line by asking why she came to Camden Cove. Luckily, she didn't clam up like the other times he'd tried asking any sort of personal questions. As he studied the crack running across the ceiling, he realized he knew absolutely nothing about her.

He tried to imagine what made Rachael need to come all the way to Camden Cove. He had so many questions, but he didn't want to push it. He might know a few new things about her, but the fact remained that he didn't really know who Rachael Hawkins was. He had searched her name. No social media, no white pages, nothing. It was as if Rachael Hawkins never existed.

CHAPTER 11

*R*achael woke to sunlight peeking through the curtains and Captain sitting up in his crate, staring at her. The moment he noticed her moving, his whole body shook and he whined. His tail wagged against the metal as he tried to stand.

"Shush, Cap." She got up and tip-toed toward his crate, opening the door. She rubbed the top of his head and his tail immediately pounded against the floor. He stretched out and licked her face.

"Good morning to you, too," she said, rubbing her cheek against his.

His tail wagged harder and he popped up from the blankets, bouncing out onto the floor, nursing his hurt leg, but having no problem walking around.

"Looks like you're feeling better." She heard movement coming from downstairs. She peeked out the window to see if there was any damage from the storm. From the window's vantage point, the backyard looked pretty good, and the fields beyond. Nothing much more than some tree branches on the ground. The power must've come back in the middle of the night, since the clock next to the bed flashed twelve, on and off.

Elizabeth had said she lived on a little farm, but as Rachael got a better look of things, it was *quite* a farm. It had acres of open fields, and even a pond. White fences ran down along the property's edge and continued down the dirt road as far as she could see.

Captain started scratching on the door to get out.

"Hold on, Captain." She grabbed her jeans and threw on a shirt. She pulled her hair up into a ponytail, then quietly opened the door. Captain hobbled down the stairs before she could stop him.

From below, she heard Captain's tail bang against something as she heard Jack say, "Hey, buddy, how are you?"

She stopped on the landing, where he couldn't see her from below, but she could hear what was happening.

"You look like you feel good," Jack continued to talk to the dog, and Captain's tail pounded faster. "Want to go outside?"

The dog's claws tapped across the floor and the door opened and shut. She hurried to the bottom floor, to watch as Jack stood outside on the back porch with Captain hobbling along in the dewy grass.

"He's not trained," Elizabeth said from behind her.

Rachael jumped, not realizing Elizabeth had come down the stairs. "Jack?"

"Yes, well, him too." Elizabeth winked, then walked into the kitchen, holding up a coffee mug. "Want some?"

"Yes, please."

"Did Captain have an accident?"

Rachael had slept heavily. Did he escape, and go somewhere in the house? She looked around Elizabeth's home, suddenly noticing her expensive furniture.

"No, but he might, and that's okay." Elizabeth put the pot under the faucet. "What I mean is that I think he's a stray. I don't think he belonged to anyone. Which means he's yours, if no one claims him."

Rachael smiled at the thought. Captain was hers. She looked out the kitchen window as Captain sniffed the ground with the other dogs. How did he survive on his own for so long? The idea of him alone and hungry broke her heart. "He's been on the streets?"

Elizabeth shrugged. "Maybe a farm dog? But if I had to guess he never had a home."

Rachael heard barking and looked out the window to see Captain romping with Elizabeth's other two dogs. Elizabeth's voice faded into the background as Rachael focused on Jack playing with the dogs.

"I know he's my brother." Elizabeth paused for a moment. "But he's also one of the greatest guys I know."

Rachael smiled, looking out at the back yard. Jack had a stick that had fallen in the storm, and threw it a few feet in front of Captain. The dog didn't move, just stood there watching Jack, then looking at the stick. Jack jumped at the stick. A laugh escaped her as his efforts to get Captain to fetch the stick failed miserably.

"I know," Rachael admitted. "It's not him, believe me."

Elizabeth handed her a cup of coffee. "My grandmother always said not to let the past control your future."

Rachael's confession sat on the tip of her tongue, but Lucy shoved the door open from outside. She wore cowboy boots and held a basket of eggs. "They all laid again!"

Rachael let out a nervous laugh, looking back out at Jack. She tried to focus on the present moment. Right then was pretty great. Maybe Elizabeth was right. She'd been so busy trying to figure out how to survive the future, even though the only thing real was right in front of her. Not her fears or her worries. Not her imaginary thoughts of Nick hunting her down.

Jack was real. His kindness was real. His family's kindness was real.

And her feelings for him were real.

If only it could be that simple. Rachael had wished all night that she could confide in Jack. Tell him everything, take some of the weight off her shoulders, but she couldn't.

Not ever.

~

Elizabeth felt her uncles' judgement as she sat in the bakery.

"All those years you gave us a hard time," Frank said, shaking his head.

David tsked. "You called us meddlesome."

"No one calls anyone meddlesome, unless you live at Pemberley." Elizabeth rolled her eyes at her uncles' dramatics. "Sometimes, you guys get a bit too involved in our lives, especially with the people we date."

Frank shrugged as though he had no idea he had crossed the line with his intrusiveness. "That's because you always choose so badly."

"What? That's not true." Her mother and uncles never liked *anyone* she or her sister or brothers or cousins dated. "Adam's perfect."

"That's because of us!" David now gave her *the look*. "Your mother needs to be involved."

"No." Elizabeth crossed her arms across her chest. "Absolutely not."

"Then we take control of some of the events." Frank sat down at the table. He was ready to get to business.

Elizabeth looked across the room at a couple she didn't recognize. She needed to be sure no one else from Camden Cove heard her plan, because it would end up spreading across town by noon.

"Rachael needs to come to Sunday dinner, first."

"She didn't seem all that interested in him," said David. "Are you sure this is a good idea?"

Frank shot him a look. "Are you kidding? Didn't you see them shoveling sand?"

"Yes..?" David looked at Elizabeth as if she'd understand what his husband meant. "I saw them shoveling sand."

"They were practically all over each other." Frank rolled his eyes.

Elizabeth pulled her croissant apart and took a bite. "I didn't see the sand shoveling." She pointed the remainder of her croissant at the two of them. "But I did see something last night, at my house."

"Last night?" Frank sat at the edge of his seat. "What happened last night?"

Elizabeth looked out the window at Jack, who stood in the parking lot of the restaurant assessing the damage from the storm. Luckily, the property seemed mostly unscathed. "Let's just say, I've never seen Jack like that before."

"You know your mother's going to kill you for not including her," warned David.

Elizabeth eyed her uncles, thinking of all the different outcomes that could arise from not including Sarah. Her mom always meant well, but tended to have loose lips. Secrets were never her forte, and Jack liked to keep his whole life a secret, a typical male trait in the Williams family. Too many people involved meant more people slipping up and exposing their plan. With Rachael being so skittish, Elizabeth didn't want to scare her off.

Elizabeth had liked her right away. Rachael felt like a long-lost friend. They talked easily and had a ton in common. She and Lucy hit it off, too. Even though Elizabeth could tell Rachael held back a lot, she still liked her dry sense of humor. There was no denying that Jack had a thing for the very pretty woman who had blown into town. Last night proved that. Even Adam saw it.

"We can only involve Sarah," Elizabeth gave in, but only on one stipulation, "if I'm the one doing the planning."

∾

When Rachael got Jack's text saying she could return to the apartment, she left Captain at Elizabeth's and took a ride into town with Adam and Lucy. They dropped her off in the restaurant parking lot and headed off to the tack store. Jack stood outside the restaurant with some men. The dock was still intact, but they examined some damage to the railings.

"Was there any water inside?" she heard the man ask, surveying the property as they all walked around to the entrance.

"No, everything looks good inside." Jack waved when he saw her. She waved back, feeling strangely shy even though she'd had breakfast with him just a couple hours ago. She looked up the street toward the tavern, which appeared unscathed. People were out helping with the cleanup. Mostly only missing shingles and destroyed gardens, but she heard some commotion about a boat that had been overturned. She was glad to see Camden Cove had survived another storm.

"We can take the storm shutters down this afternoon." The man with Jack pointed to the windows. "Then bring the sand to the dump. I'll go and grab the trailer."

Jack looked around with his hands on his hips. "We're lucky there's only a little clean up."

Rachael spoke up. "I could help salvage most of the flowers and decorations in the containers."

Most of the fall chrysanthemums and gourds and pumpkins had survived the storm, even after being blown into the streets. She'd have to reshape and prune most of the mums and toss a few pumpkins, but the purple cabbage and larger pumpkins still looked good.

"That would be great," Jack said, his lips looking as luscious as the night before. She had to look away, feeling her cheeks warm.

"Remind me to call our landscapers," the man said to Jack.

"Rachael, have you met my father?"

She recognized the man from the wedding. "You gave the speech."

He beamed as he held out his hand. "John Williams. I heard you're Finn's granddaughter."

Jack jaw dropped. "You're Finn's granddaughter?"

She didn't know what to say, surprised that his father knew about their relationship. As far as she knew, no one knew Finn was her grandfather, besides her and Finn. Had Finn told John?

"Yes, well, we just sort of reconnected." She looked back at Jack, who seemed confused. She had been vague, but was that sort of lying, too? She waved again and said, "I'm going to grab some stuff before I head to work."

As she ran up the stairs, she wondered if she should've opened up about Finn. Maybe she should have told him everything, even about Nick. Then she thought about how they sat on the couch playing cards into the middle of the night. How he scooped Captain up in his arms and took him out.

It wasn't until she reached for a light switch that she noticed how dark the whole place was, with the storm shutters over all the windows, and instant panic set in. Her heart pounded with it. She shook her head at herself. What was getting into her?

The silence encompassed her, even the waves' gentle hum couldn't be heard. She couldn't shake the strange feeling. It was just her imagination, she thought, as a cool draft swept by her. She swung around, trying to figure out where it came from, noticing she had left the door ajar. A slant of light came in. That's what was different. Barely any natural light came inside, except in long slits along the floor.

Hadn't she left all the lights on?

"Hello?" Rachael called out. She grabbed the baseball bat she had found in the closet and held it up, ready to swing. She knew she had left all the lights on. She **always** left the lights on. The storm may have taken the power out, but some of the lights should have turned back on when the power returned. The switches had been physically shut off. Her hand shook nervously as she flipped the light switch in the bathroom. Nothing. No one.

"Hey."

"Ahh!" She swung the bat, just missing Jack's stomach.

Jack held out his hands. "I'm sorry I startled you. You okay?"

"Someone went into my apartment." She dropped the bat to her side.

"Oh, yeah, I did. I hope that's alright, I needed to see if there was any damage."

"No, it's not alright." Her words were sharp and harsher than she intended. Anger brewed inside. "You don't just go into someone's apartment without asking them."

"I'm sorry." Jack walked toward her.

"You didn't ask my permission to go into my apartment." She stepped back away from him.

"You're right." He shook his head. "I'm really sorry. I should've asked first."

"You didn't need to go around and shut off all my lights, either."

"I didn't touch any of your lights."

"What?" Her heart dropped. "You didn't turn off the lights?"

"It was probably just the storm."

"No, it wasn't the storm." Rachael's throat dried up. Her eyes darted around, checking her surroundings. How long ago had Nick been there? Was he around, right now? Watching from afar? She bit her bottom lip.

Jack's face became concerned. "Do you think someone went inside the apartment besides me?"

"You're sure you didn't turn off the lights?"

Jack thought about it. "I don't think I did, but now I don't know."

She looked back at the apartment.

"Did you notice anything missing?" he asked

"I don't have anything."

"People know the houses on the beach will be empty with the storm. I'll just call my buddy who's an officer in town, I could—"

She grabbed his phone.

"What are you doing?"

"I don't want you to call the police."

"You probably just turned them off when you left the night of the storm, and forgot. I can check to see if anything's missing."

He tried to step further into the apartment, but she blocked him. She could barely look at him. He didn't see the problem at all. Her privacy, her space, meant nothing to him.

"Are you okay?"

"You should leave."

"Come on, Rachael, I meant no harm. I honestly was just checking for damage." He rubbed his forehead waiting for her to respond, but she didn't. He reached for the door, and stopped. "Rachael, what's going on? What are you running away from?"

"It's just better if you go." She stood there and waited for him to leave, then locked the door behind him.

CHAPTER 12

*E*lizabeth stood at the counter as Mrs. Corbet, with Mr. Wheezy in her arms, rambled on about how the town selectmen had their heads up their "you know whats".

"And if Bill Milner doesn't stop with the 'years of service'," Margie jumped in. "He just does it so he can have a night away from Susan."

"Don't I know it?" Mrs. Corbet clicked her tongue. "They just like all the special events because they get free drinks."

Margie nodded in agreement.

Elizabeth wanted to say the same thing to Mrs. Corbet, who also sat on the board of selectmen, enjoying the same free meals, but she stayed quiet. Even if they made some of the strangest decisions, like the ban on roller skates at the beach, as if someone would roller skate in the sand. But in the end, even Bill Milner put his heart and soul into the voluntary position.

Through the window, Elizabeth noticed Rachael walking up the street. Her plan for Jack and Rachael could begin early, she thought, as she watched her walk toward the clinic. She'd invite Rachael to the annual Harvest Festival downtown, and "get an emergency call", having to leave her all alone with Jack. He would've worked the restaurant, but he always closed by the time of the dance.

Elizabeth met Rachael at the door as she walked in. "How did the apartment fare in the storm?"

"Fine." Rachael smiled, but it faded quickly.

Something was wrong. "You okay?"

"Can we talk?" Rachael looked over to the two older women staring at them. "Maybe somewhere private?"

"Yes, let's go into the examination room." Elizabeth ushered Rachael into the small room across the lobby.

Elizabeth shut the door behind Rachael. When she looked back at her, she could see her face twisting as though she held back tears. She reached out and took her hand.

"What's going on, Rachael?"

"I need you to keep Captain, after all." A tear fell and she quickly swiped it away, pulling her shoulders back. "And find him a new family."

Elizabeth couldn't believe what she was hearing. Rachael loved that dog. "What are you talking about?"

She took off her backpack and set it down on top of the examination table. "These are all of his things. I can pay for his stay here until you find a family, but could you please take him?"

"Of course." She leaned down to catch Rachael's eye. "But stop for a second, and tell me what's gotten you so upset?"

Rachael stood up and closed her eyes. Two tears fell in unison down her cheeks. "I have to leave."

"What?" Elizabeth placed her hands gently on Rachael's arms. "Why do you have to leave?"

Rachael blew out a breath, then in a low voice said, "I just need to leave."

Elizabeth wasn't going to take vague answers anymore. "Sit down and tell me what's going on."

Rachael looked like she was going to argue, but then took a seat in the chair. Elizabeth held her hand.

"What's got you so spooked?" Elizabeth only had one guess,

with the way Rachael came to town. With all the things Jack had told her.

"I think someone went into my apartment while I stayed at your place."

"Seriously?" Elizabeth had lived in Camden Cove her whole life and could only think of a few instances where someone's house was broken into. "Did you call the police?"

She shook her head. "I can't."

"Why?" Elizabeth understood why she'd be nervous about staying alone, especially if she thought someone had been there. "You don't have to leave. Jack can install an alarm in the apartment if you're concerned. You can stay with us until you're comfortable."

"An alarm won't work." Rachael shook her head. "That won't stop him."

Elizabeth heard the pronoun. "Stop who?"

Rachael took back her hands, her thumbs rubbing the inside of her palms. "I need to get away from someone."

"Who?"

"My husband."

Rachael listened as Adam talked on his phone. She picked at a string hanging out of the corner of a placemat as he spoke about her situation. Elizabeth sat next to her at the table, her attention on Adam, who spoke about filing a motion for divorce. Rachael rubbed her fingers against the smooth oak top, remembering the last time she sat at the table. She had felt completely at ease, sitting around with Elizabeth's family and Jack. Now, her anxiety revved with every heartbeat pounding inside her chest.

"Maggie has a little cabin on the property for staff." Elizabeth had showed her the website of a rehabilitation farm. The farm had mostly horses, but also other animals who needed help. The irony that Rachael would work with abused animals didn't escape her. "She's been looking for someone for some time, can't seem to keep much in the way of farm hands these days. It's hard work, but it's a beautiful farm, and Maggie's one of the best around."

Rachael wasn't so sure she believed that Maggie had been looking for someone, but for the time being, she had no other choice. She needed to leave, whether Nick went into the apartment or not. She had depended on Jack and his generosity for too long.

Adam put his phone in his pocket and returned to the table. "Did you ever call the police when you were with Nick?"

"Once, but he wasn't charged. I doubt there was any record of the call."

That night had been one of the worst times with Nick. She was sure he was going to kill her. Somehow, she managed to call 911 and leave the phone off the hook. When the police showed up to the house, the two officers knew Nick. They spent the night cooling him down and convincing her not to press charges because of his career. They had promised to help her, but had only helped Nick.

"Did you go to the hospital for any of your injuries?"

"Yes." She knew she could've gone to a judge, brought her medical papers showing all the injuries she had been treated for over the years, but she doubted that any judge would believe her over Nick. She had covered it up, lying to the medical personnel about how she got hurt. Only one emergency room nurse, who had recognized her after her third visit, had asked about her situation at home without Nick standing over her shoulder. At that point, she should've said something, but the nurse would've given herself away once Nick returned to the room. Somehow she'd give him a look, or act differently in front of him, and at that point Rachael wasn't sure what he'd do to her.

"I only went to the hospital a few times." Her voice was small. Shame washed over her as Elizabeth grabbed her hand. What kind of person didn't stand up for themselves? What did that say about her as a person?

"Many women don't tell how they get their injuries," Adam said, as though he could read her mind. "They know the repercussions are too great."

Adam's phone started to ding. He grabbed a legal pad and began scribbling notes. He walked to the table and sat across from Rachael.

"We're going to call all the places you were treated and get records. Once we get everything, we can start by filing a motion to a judge for a divorce, and a new social security card. They will be discreet if we can prove you're concerned for your safety. If we can show you called the police station that night and they came out, then I'm sure a judge will help you."

Rachael started shaking her head before he finished his sentence. "What if he finds out, he'll come looking for me. Nick's not the kind of guy who will just let me leave him."

"That's why you're going to Maggie's. No one except for Elizabeth and me will know where you are."

"But he'll know I've come this far. He could come after you."

"He's not that stupid." Adam shook his head. "I can even send another attorney down to represent you. Giving another degree of separation."

"I can't afford this." Rachael twisted her hand so hard she no longer could feel it.

"A new social security number could mean you can get your own bank accounts, credit records, and get away from Nick for good." Elizabeth reached for her hand.

Rachael shook her head. "I don't think that'll ever happen."

Adam leaned forward in his seat, the wood cracking underneath his weight. "Rachael, you can't afford not to."

She nodded.

"I can bring you tomorrow, if you're ready to go," Elizabeth said.

Rachael looked over at Captain, lying with the other dogs. "I just need to do one thing before we leave."

She knocked on Finn's door an hour later.

"What you doing here?" he asked, instead of inviting her in.

"I needed to say goodbye." She wasn't going to beat around the bush.

"I have dinner for Sunday." He looked upset that she would be ruining his plans.

She smiled and handed him an envelope with her letter inside. "Thanks for giving me a job."

He pushed it back. "You can't leave now. You just started figuring out how to fill the paper orders."

She reached out and wrapped her hand around his forearm, squeezing it. "I will call you when I'm settled."

He huffed. "Did that Jack Williams raise the rent on you?"

She shook her head. "It's time for me to move along."

He walked back into the house and slammed the door on her. Frozen in shock, she stared at the door and watched him through the window. He walked through to the dining room and straight out the back door. She heard the screen door slam shut. Then he started up his truck, backing it down the driveway. She watched the whole thing from the porch.

He cut the engine and got out. "Well, you'll need to get some gas, but you should be able to get where you need to go with this truck."

Her mouth fell open. "I couldn't."

He climbed the porch steps, handing her the keys. "Just promise me you'll call when you can."

She walked over and embraced him. "Thanks, Pop."

He only patted her back before stepping away. "You're going to be okay, Rach."

∼

The whole next day at the restaurant, Jack perseverated on his reaction with Rachael about the apartment. She was rightfully upset that he had gone inside her apartment. He should've asked. What was he thinking? His mind couldn't focus for more than a second. He wanted to go up to her apartment so badly, to apologize, but what would be the point? She'd never trust him again. How could he have been so stupid?

He needed to fix things. He'd leave her alone, but after he apologized. When he finally got up the nerve to go up, tell her how sorry he was, Elizabeth walked in the back door of the restaurant with Captain on his leash.

He knelt down and rubbed the dog's neck. "Where's Rachael?"

"Well, I've had an interesting couple of days." She bent down to Captain, who sat happily between them. His mouth opened wide in a doggy smile, even though his leg was still bandaged up. "Look, I'm not supposed to tell you, but..."

"What?" His stomach dropped to the hard floor.

"Rachael left."

"She left? Where'd she go?"

She shook her head. "I can't tell you."

"You can't tell me? Are you serious?"

Elizabeth gave him that look she did when she felt sorry for him. "Look Jack, she isn't something you can fix."

"What's that supposed to mean?" Jack crossed his arms.

"She doesn't need your help."

"She obviously needs help."

"That may be true, but she has to be willing to accept it." She sounded strangely reasonable, which annoyed him.

"So, I just have to sit by and know she's in trouble?" he almost growled at her.

"No, you have to sit by..." She handed over the leash, "And take care of Captain."

"Where is she, Elizabeth?"

She made the *sorry* face again. "I promised not to tell you."

"This isn't high school."

Elizabeth let out a long sigh as she stood up. "It's like what mom always said, you can't cross the monkey bars without letting go."

"What do monkey bars have to do with anything?" He didn't have time for nursery rhymes.

"It means you care enough to let her go, so she can get to the other side on her own." Elizabeth stood up. "If you can't take care of Captain, I can start looking for another home for him."

Jack shook his head, scowling at his sister and her advice. What had Rachael told her? "I can take care of Captain. I just don't understand why you can't tell me where she is."

She handed him an envelope. He looked inside, at the brass key he had given to Rachael.

"Is she okay?" he asked.

She nodded. "Yes, she'll be okay."

She left after that. Good riddance, too, because that was all he could take in the way of sisterly advice at the moment. Who was she trying to be, Oprah? Because it wasn't working. He ran upstairs to the apartment to see for himself. The place was empty. She was really gone.

As Jack brought Captain back to his house, his annoyance with Rachael grew for taking off without saying a thing, and his anger with Elizabeth grew for holding to her word. He may have crossed the line with going into her apartment, but he had apologized for that. If he had been a jerk to her in the past, maybe he'd understand why she was so repulsed by him, but his reasoning for going in the apartment was legit. The least she could've done was to give back the key in person, not in some envelope given to his sister.

He turned his annoyance back to Elizabeth. She just expected him to swallow the fact that Rachael took her help after everything he had done, and then to take care of Captain, to top it all off? Was he that much of a sucker?

Then he looked down at Captain. Rachael wouldn't have just

given Captain up, unless something made her. What was she hiding?

"What are we going to do, Captain?" The dog looked back at him as though he was going to answer.

He drove home and practically parked in the bushes, because of Matt's crummy job of parking in the driveway. Captain pulled him through the thorns, scraping his arms up. He cursed the few roses still hanging on. There hadn't been a frost yet, but it would be coming soon, and the roses would die. Nothing lasted. He laughed bitterly, almost sneering as he thought about all the relationships that had turned cold in his life. He had thought he felt the way his father had on the day he laid eyes on his mother. God, how many times had he drunk to that speech?

When he opened the sliding glass door, he heard a woman's voice. He looked around and saw a jacket on the back of a kitchen chair, a purse on the table, and a pair of jeans on the floor.

He turned the corner to the living room and saw Matt, standing with only a couch cushion covering himself.

"What the...?" Jack said. Captain instantly went into hyper mode and started barking at Matt.

"I thought you were at work." Matt looked sheepishly at him.

Jack looked out the front window and noticed the now-familiar car in the road. "Are you kidding me?" he gestured toward the window. "You're sleeping with Justine?"

"She *is* my wife," Matt's voice held an edge.

Jack didn't care if he made Matt upset or not. He was making the biggest mistake of his life. "I have only two words: Freddy Harrington."

Matt's eyes narrowed. "That's a cheap shot, Jack."

Jack shrugged. "It's the truth."

Matt shook his head. "I think it's best I be on my way."

"I agree. Lucky for you, there's an available apartment." He threw the key at him and it bounced off the cushion.

Matt walked over to the brass key, bent down and picked it

up. Then he walked up to Jack and held out his hand dropping his cushion.

Jack huffed, "What?"

"A bet's a bet." Matt's hand reached out further. "You owe me two hundred dollars."

～

"Thank you so much for letting me come tonight," Rachael said to Maggie, the owner of the farm where she was now a resident. She looked around the small cabin and couldn't believe how once again she was indebted to the Williams. Once again she promised herself she'd pay them back somehow. Elizabeth and Adam had done so much for her, she should've been more grateful, but sorrow filled her chest. How did Jack react to her leaving? Was he upset? Or relieved?

"Sure thing." Maggie stood in a pair of rubber boots and a baseball cap and pulled the rest of the sheets off the furniture. "I always need an extra hand around the farm."

She flipped on all the lights and walked around the room. It wasn't much larger than the apartment above the restaurant, but perfect for her. Rachael suddenly wished she had said goodbye to Jack. But she knew if she had, he'd just try to convince her to stay, and she couldn't risk it.

"There's a small bedroom through that door and a bathroom around the corner, which only has a tub." The woman put her hands on her hips. She looked like she was in her fifties, or maybe early sixties. Her long gray hair hung down in a braid, just like the horses out in the fields.

"Thank you, it's perfect." Rachael didn't move from the entrance. She wondered how much Elizabeth had told her. Enough for the woman to agree to have Rachael move in. "Thanks again for everything."

"Adam and Elizabeth have helped me out more than once. If you need anything, don't be a stranger."

Rachael nodded.

"The closest grocery store is… nowhere close." Maggie chuckled at her own joke. "But I've got some essentials you can have for the time being."

"I'll be fine," Rachael said. "I'm not that hungry anyway."

Rachael's stomach had twisted in knots through the whole ride to New Hampshire. Even though it was less than an hour away from Camden Cove, she felt nauseated at the idea of not knowing where she was going, or not being able to plan out her next move. Would this be her life? Always in constant anxiety of what lurked around the corner? Would she be in this same position, again and again?

"I heard you had a dog?" Maggie asked. "Plenty of space for it to run around here."

A pang hit her in the chest. She didn't want to think about Captain. Elizabeth had tried to insist that Rachael keep Captain, but she couldn't be on the move with a dog. Maggie might be cool with her having a dog, but most rentals were not on a farm in the country. Besides, one thing she knew for sure, Jack would take care of him.

"Thanks, I'll keep that in mind." Rachael plastered on a smile as best as she could. The day she left Nick, she had been as scared as she was right now, except then she also had a sliver of hope that she was gaining her freedom. Now, even though she couldn't have asked for a better situation — no one within miles, no one except for Elizabeth, Adam and Maggie knowing where she was — she felt more trapped than ever.

Maggie didn't stay long and after she left, Rachael checked out the small cabin, thinking of when she first moved in with Nick. It had been the first time she had left home, left her mom. She couldn't wait to have her own place and be able to decorate the way she wanted. Nick promised she could start as soon as they got married.

Even after he first hit her, she still browsed the home decoration sections in department stores and leafed through home and garden magazines, dreaming up color schemes.

As cute as the little cabin was, the wood paneling of twelve-inch pine, the tiny wood stove, the loft overhead, she didn't care about any of it. She didn't have it in her to ever look at this place as a home. And she feared she'd never have a home again. The last thing Nick promised her was that he'd kill her before he let her leave him. And she believed him.

She decided not to unpack. Instead, she hung her backpack off the hook on the closet door. A knock on the door made her jump and Maggie peeked in the inset window.

"I've made you dinner," she spoke through the door.

Rachael rushed over and opened the door. "You didn't have to make me dinner."

She held a casserole dish in her hands. "I hope you like chicken." She removed the tinfoil cover, revealing roasted chicken and vegetables.

"That looks amazing." Rachael hadn't noticed how hungry she really was until she had smelled the rich steam rising up from the dish. "Really, I can't accept all this."

"You'll pay me back with your work." Maggie placed it on the table.

"Deal." Rachael nodded. "Thank you."

"There's plates in the cabinet and silverware in that drawer by the sink," Maggie pointed to the cupboards.

Rachael pushed wisps of hair away from her eyes and looked at the large amount of food. "Have you and your family had dinner, yet?"

Maggie shook her head. "All my chickens grew up and flew the coup, I'm afraid." Rachael noticed that she rubbed the ring on her finger. "It's just me and the animals."

"Would you like to join me for dinner?" Rachael gestured to the table. Maggie hesitated. "Unless of course, you have somewhere else to be."

"I'd love to join you." Maggie smiled. "I can show you where everything is."

"Perfect."

Maggie headed straight to the kitchen and started pulling plates out from the cabinets, along with two glasses. She placed everything on the table as Rachael grabbed the silverware. "Have you worked a farm before?"

Rachael made a face and shook her head. "No, I'm afraid not."

Maggie smiled, but something in her eyes made Rachael think that Elizabeth had shared her story. Why else would she take in someone with no experience?

"People either love working a farm, or they hate it." Maggie filled the water glasses and handed one to Rachael. "To new beginnings."

Rachael clanked her glass against Maggie's, but her new beginning had already ended when she left Camden Cove.

～

All day and night, Jack moped around the restaurant. When he finally got home and went to bed, he just stared at the ceiling. He even let Captain up on his bed with him, but the dog took over most of the space and made sleeping impossible. After tossing and turning, he headed downstairs.

The house felt empty without Matt, who left two hundred dollars richer. He hadn't wasted any time moving into the apartment. He didn't even notice when Justine slithered away. He didn't even want to think of the possibility of those two getting back together. The idea brought back the familiar guilt he hoped would've disappeared after he discovered Justine and Freddy. He should've told Matt right away, when things happened. Maybe Matt already knew. Justine would certainly enjoy ruining another relationship.

He looked out the windows at the water. He had dreamed of living on the water like this since he was a kid. When the McGibbons told his parents they were headed down to Florida for retirement, he put in an offer, a generous one, too.

His little cottage had been everything he had ever wanted, two decent bedrooms, a great kitchen, and the best view in all of Camden Cove. Perfect for a single guy who lived for his work.

From the sliding doors, he could see the curve of the cove and at its very end, the restaurant. He had felt such pride in the restaurant and the house. But now he felt nothing but lonely.

Captain whined at the door. He leashed him up and took him outside. He needed to do something other than sit in that house as the rest of the world carried on as normal.

Captain took off toward the restaurant.

"Come on, Cap, she's not there." Jack spoke to the dog as if he understood. Then he mumbled, "I feel the same way."

The morning dragged on, and he headed to work. Captain needed to rest the leg, but he didn't have the heart to crate him, so he brought the dog with him. He'd keep him in his office. When he pulled up into his spot, Matt opened the apartment door in his fishing gear.

"Got any company?" Jack said sarcastically, as he unlocked the back door.

Matt stopped at the bottom of the stairs and huffed. "Really?"

Jack decided not to push it any further. By Matt's demeanor, he could tell he was ready to fight. "So, you're in the apartment, then?"

Matt bent down and rubbed behind Captain's ear. "I am."

"Good."

"Good."

A silent agreement settled between the two brothers.

"You should come out with me today," Matt said.

"I can't." Jack shook his head. "I have the restaurant to open."

"You have a ton of employees that you hired for that kind of thing," Matt argued. He pulled on the rim of his baseball cap. "One day isn't going to kill you. In fact, one day on the water is exactly what you need."

White clouds hung on the surface of the water. "I get to bring Captain."

Matt looked at the dog. "He'll do."

Jack texted his sous chef, Michael, that he'd be out for the day, and to take care of things. In all the years working at the restaurant, he had never called in to blow off work. But as he followed his little brother down to the docks, where Matt's lobster boat was moored, he wanted nothing more than to get away from Camden Cove.

He looked at Matt. A water baby was what their mother had called him, but maybe the water was Matt's secret to being able to handle all the things life has thrown at him. Jack could hardly complain that a woman who wanted nothing to do with him in the first place, left town. Especially when his brother, whose marriage was as rocky as the Maine coast, seemed completely fine with life.

He climbed aboard and stood inside the wheelhouse as Matt started the engine, doing his normal rituals like all fishermen did. He switched the radio on first, then pulled the five-gallon bucket off the exhaust, then switching on the fish finder. When everything was prepared to go, Matt guided the boat out to sea and Jack watched as Camden Cove disappeared.

Matt steered up the coast to his regular fishing spot, the waters around Perkins Island. The same territory their grandfather had fished when he was alive, and their great grandfather before that. The rocky coastline was a kaleidoscope of fall colors, from bright oranges to peachy yellows and deep shades of burgundy. Fall had officially peaked.

Matt slowed the boat down and cut the engine. He headed out on the deck, getting to work. With a hook, he caught hold of the buoy and pulled the rope up onto the electric pulley.

"How many pots do you have in the water?" Jack asked as he grabbed the rope, helping Matt to pull it up alongside the boat.

"About two hundred." Matt dropped the trap onto the deck.

And just like when they were kids, the two brothers pulled the lobster out of the traps and measured them, tossing the good ones in the tank and throwing out the small ones, or the ones with eggs. Captain watched as they tossed the lobster back in and whined, wanting to jump overboard and catch them, but soon, he too was lulled by the waves.

The rhythm of the work cleared Jack's mind. He grabbed another bait bag and dumped in the herring.

"You haven't lost your touch with chum," Matt teased. "I'm sorry about yesterday."

Jack nodded. "I'm sorry, too."

Matt shrugged. "I don't know what I was thinking."

"You can say that again," Jack mumbled under his breath.

"I thought you just apologized?"

Jack held up the herring bag. "Sorry, man, I just don't want her to hurt you all over again."

"She may have made mistakes, but I made just as many along the way."

"You slept with Freddy Harrington?"

"No, but I wasn't a good husband." Matt stuffed his own bait bag. "The fact is, it takes two people to make a marriage work, and I wasn't there for the right reasons."

"Then why are you sleeping with her?" Jack didn't understand.

Matt shrugged again. "I don't know. I mean, deep down I love her, and I guess I always will. We're just terrible for one another."

"Freddy's going to find out." If Jack had noticed Justine's car parked in the road, it wouldn't take long for people to put two and two together.

"Well, that would be just an added bonus." Matt shook his head as he grabbed the bait bag from Jack and threw it into the trap, slamming it shut. He threw it over the side.

"How long have you been sleeping with her?"

Matt gave him a look like he was done with the conversation. He went back to his spot in the wheelhouse, but didn't start up the engine.

"You going to just let her leave?" Matt asked.

Jack made a face, not sure what his brother meant.

Matt lifted an eyebrow. "Rachael."

"What am I going to do, chase after her?" Jack shook his head. "You got your money."

"Doesn't Dad always talk about how he chased the girl?"

"It's way more complicated than that." Jack didn't want to talk about his troubles with women. He sat in the captain's chair, holding the wheel while the dog lay on the floor next to his feet. He tried to change the topic. "Don't you want to head up the shore toward Pleasant Point?"

"I don't think it's more complicated," Matt said, as though he had thought about it. "I think you just have to be willing to let go."

"What? Have you been talking to Elizabeth?"

"You can't control everything."

"I'm not trying to."

"Are you kidding me?" Matt laughed at his brother. "You always have to control the situation, even on my boat."

Jack looked at the wheel and slumped further down into the captain's chair. "I just wanted to help her."

"Does she want *your* help?" Matt let out an exaggerated sigh. "I mean, does she know you have a thing for her, or does she think you just feel sorry for her?"

Jack gave his brother a look. He hated when he was right. "I don't have a thing."

"Look, I'm the last person to give advice." Matt scratched his head. "But maybe you should chase the girl, instead of using her situation to *get* the girl."

"Maybe you shouldn't sleep with the girl to get the girl," Jack snapped back.

"Touché." Matt smiled. "But I'm not trying to deny I'm in love with the girl."

Jack was about to argue. Love? Hardly. Right? He leaned

further back, blowing out a long breath. "She doesn't even want to talk to me. She told Elizabeth not to tell me where she is."

"So? When has that stopped you before?"

"I don't want to mess things up again."

"If I'm being completely honest here, you're going to mess it up anyways." Matt smiled, clearly joking, but patted him on the back. He pulled Jack out from the chair, taking back his seat as he turned the engine. "Go for the girl, man."

It didn't take Rachael long to learn the ropes at the farm. If you can work hard, use every muscle in your body, and be able to hold out all day, you can work a farm. First thing, even before the rooster crowed, she hit the barn. Maggie had explained what she needed to do the night before after dinner, and Rachael certainly didn't need advice on how to clean up a mess. She had been doing that since she was a kid. She opened the barn doors for the goats and sheep, feeling more at ease with them than the horses and cows. By the time she cleaned out the chicken coop, Rachael heard the screen door slam, and the tramping of three dogs.

"Sadie, don't you bother the girls!" Maggie called out as she rounded the corner. She wore the same pair of rubber boots and her Red Sox cap, her braid hanging down her back. "That little sassafras."

A dog, who must've been Sadie, ran toward the chickens with total disregard. She ran right into the flock. Squawking chickens fluttered about the yard, feathers floating around them as the dog romped around, tongue out, trying to play with them.

Rachael wished she had brought Captain. He'd have a blast, but she knew he was in good hands.

"Come help me in the fields." Maggie threw a pair of gloves at her. "Grab a couple of shovels, and I'll meet you out back with the four-wheeler."

Rachael pulled the doors apart and stepped into the old red

barn. She felt like she was stepping into Charlotte's Web, expecting to see Wilbur peeking over the stall door. The sun came in through the windows. Rays of light illuminated floating dust motes. The scent of toasted hay hung in the air.

She grabbed two shovels and headed out toward the engine rumbling outside. Maggie sat in an ATV 4x4 with a trailer hitched to the back.

"I got this for my sixtieth birthday." Maggie patted the empty seat next to her. Rachael dropped the shovels in the back of the trailer.

"Should I grab a helmet?" asked Rachael, climbing into the seat.

"Naw, I hardly drive faster than I walk. But if you get in with the baby of the family, Rosie, watch your blessed stars, because she's the devil on this thing."

Rachael smiled at the thought of a wild-haired young Maggie, hitting the world with fire trailing behind her. "I bet she's a good time."

"Ah, yes, apparently she is," Maggie sighed. She hit the gas and headed out toward the field behind the barn. Two ruts created a path that curved through an orchard of apple trees, passed a stone wall, then wound up a hill and out of view. The road had protruding rocks, which Maggie slowed down for like an expert. "I have to fix the southern fence before winter. A post rotted out. We'll dig it up and replace it with a new one."

As the fall colors blurred by on the way to the broken fence, she promised to repay Maggie back, just like she promised she'd pay back Elizabeth and Adam, Frank and David and of course, Finn.

And Jack.

She wanted so badly to be able to show up at the restaurant and tell him she was okay. Back on her own two feet, not the same girl who stepped into the restaurant that rainy night. She imagined she'd wear something nice, something more than jeans and a t-shirt. She'd find something flattering and sophisticated.

Mostly she wished she'd be able to go back to Camden Cove one day and have a real home. Maybe one of those little fishing capes. No, she'd never be able to afford a house, much less go back there again. She had already stayed too long. The whole town could identify her if a police officer from out of town started asking questions. Nick might not have gone into her apartment. Jack was probably right about the storm, but something was off. She felt it.

Maggie dipped the ATV down a small hill. Golden mountain peaks lined the horizon as the sun crept above the tree line. Rachael looked back over to the orchard and the house. The farm had acres of Christmas trees planted along the rolling hills.

"This is quite a farm."

Maggie smiled and then took in a deep breath as she closed her eyes while still driving. Rachael almost grabbed the wheel, but Maggie opened her eyes again. "I lived in the city until I met Sam."

"How long have you been here?"

"I was twenty when I came, so over forty years." Maggie slowed to a stop. She grabbed the shovels from the trailer and handed one over to Rachael.

Rachael was impressed that someone Maggie's age would still be doing this kind of work on her own. She also wondered if Maggie's ring was Sam's.

"When the girls left, I've had to hire out this work," Maggie explained.

"Must've been hard to leave, with this view," Rachael said as they walked through the trees, planted in straight lines, all perfectly trimmed. Along the property, maples leaves dotted the evergreens and ground. The air filled with the smell of Christmas and drying leaves. Up above, a screech from a hawk caught her attention and she looked up, letting the sun hit her face. "I thought this was a rehabilitation farm?"

"Yes, but I also sell apples on the weekends in the fall, Christmas trees in the winter, and maple syrup in spring."

Maggie let out a huff when she spaded the dirt. "I sure did get spellbound when I moved here. I'm holding on to it for my girls, even though they want nothing to do with it, just hoping for someone to change their mind."

Rachael felt a bit jealous of Maggie's children. She loved her mother, but her mother always had more problems in her life than she could deal with. Her choices usually caused more problems. She also thought Rachael should 'hold on' to Nick, no matter what.

"Did you run your mouth?" her mother asked, the first time Rachael came back home. "What did you do to make him so angry?"

Rachael shook her thoughts away and sliced through the ground with the shovel's blade, tearing up the earth around the post. In no time, they had reached down to the rotten bottom. Maggie stood back and watched her dig.

"You sure liked that," she said with a smile.

"Yes." Rachael breathed heavily. "Yes, I liked that very much."

"Well, good. We'll find another one after this."

By the end of the day, they had fixed two posts, cut down a rotten apple tree, split the wood, and dragged it back to the barn. By the end of the day, every inch of her body hurt. All she wanted to do was to take a warm bath and go to bed. But she loved every minute of it.

"Tomorrow we'll run to town and grab supplies." Maggie put away a set of trimmers. "In the meantime, feel free to come in the house and take what you need. I still have some extras from lunch."

Rachael had enough leftovers from the previous night to satisfy her. "I'm all set."

Maggie nodded. "Well then, I'm pooped. I'll see you in the morning."

Rachael said goodnight and watched as Maggie and the dogs headed inside. The sage paint was starting to peel from the farmhouse and the shutters looked like they needed to be rehung, but

Maggie's place sure was beautiful. A swing hung from the ceiling on the side porch, overlooking the fields. Rachael imagined what life would have been like, growing up here. She'd never leave. That's for sure.

After a long bath, she grabbed a Nora Roberts off the shelf by the wood stove and curled underneath the blankets. A chill hung in the air. She rested the book on her chest and looked out at the dark night. What were Jack and Captain doing? Were they together? Did they think about her?

And would she ever stop thinking of them?

~

Jack and Captain looked out the window at the stars hanging over the water in the dark. The rhythm of the waves lulled Jack into a funk he couldn't explain. A numbness he couldn't shake and didn't want to. He wanted to be alone, except for Captain. He wanted to figure out what was going on with Rachael. He also wanted to see her, beg her to come back.

He rocked in his recliner, back and forth, not sure how long he had been sitting there. Long enough not to care anymore.

His phone buzzed on the coffee table, lighting up the room with a dull blue, another attempt from Matt to get him out of the house and meet at the Tavern. Jack turned his phone off. He wasn't up for Camden Cove drama. He was much happier sitting in his own misery than hearing the same old complaints from the same old people.

Nothing was going to make him happy until he saw her again.

He needed to see her again.

He grabbed his phone and turned it back on. He texted Elizabeth and waited, staring at the screen. Dots flashed, and soon a message popped up.

No.

I need to see her, he texted back.

I promised her I wouldn't tell you where she was, she wrote back.

Why?

The dots flickered, but then disappeared. Jack immediately opened his contacts and dialed Elizabeth's number.

"Because she doesn't want you following her and worrying about her, anymore."

"Tell me where she is, Elizabeth, please."

She let out a long sigh. "Jack, I can't."

"Why not?"

"Because knowing you, you'd go tonight, and that's not a good idea for anyone."

CHAPTER 13

$\mathcal{J}$ack walked straight to the bar after he called Finn.

"Well, you took long enough," Finn grumbled.

'You talked to her?" Jack waited for what he came for.

Finn passed over a small post-it with an address written on it. "She's working over at some farm."

Jack grabbed the piece of paper. Holly Lane Farm, Profile Falls, New Hampshire. "When did she call?"

"This morning." Finn stacked a set of coasters. "You go over there and bring her back home."

Jack gave Finn a look, holding up the post-it. "She's not going to listen to me."

The old man mumbled something under his breath as he wiped the counter with a dishtowel. "So, you just going to stand there?"

"Do you know what's going on with Rachael?" Jack asked.

"I don't ask questions!"

"You're her grandfather." Jack didn't think it was unreasonable for him to ask.

"All I know is, she's running from something."

Jack worried that that was exactly what Rachael was doing. He thanked Finn again, then received a text from Elizabeth.

"You can't go barreling over to New Hampshire without thinking things through, first," she said as soon as he answered.

"How'd?" Where did she get her information?

"Meet me at the bakery in twenty." She hung up. He tried calling her back, but it went straight to voicemail. He didn't have time to dawdle around to hear the 'What Would Elizabeth Do?' spiel. He needed to get moving. Then he looked at the post-it.

What was she running from?

Or who?

Elizabeth grabbed the bag she had packed before leaving for the bakery. Even though she planned to meet Jack, she had been going to the bakery before work as her regular routine. It was killing her thighs. Not that she wanted to be one of those women who were concerned about every pound and every inch. She had lost a bunch of weight for the wedding, after all. Yes, walking would be a good way to offset some of her indulgences.

The usual group of old men sat around by the windows, near the table she enjoyed. She sat happily listening as they veered off local politics to the weather. They all agreed that the football team would make the finals.

Jack had called like she suspected he would, but she knew him well enough to know he would be there soon. Picking apart her cinnamon roll, she sipped her warm pumpkin spiced tea as Jack's truck pulled up in front of the bakery.

She took a bite as he jumped out. She saw Captain stick his head out of the truck's window, but he stayed put as Jack walked through the door like a man on a mission. He was crazy if he thought she'd hand over the information about Rachael without an intervention. Last night, after her conversation with Jack, she had called her uncles and asked what to do. They all agreed that they needed to talk to him first before he did anything rash.

As soon as he got to the table, Frank made his way over to them. David managed the front.

"So?" Jack asked, thrusting one hand toward her.

"Sit down," she demanded.

"Stop this, Elizabeth. I know where she is, Finn told me."

"That *squealer*!" Frank hissed.

"What's so important that I needed to see you?" His patience was thin, she could tell.

"We think it's best we help you," Elizabeth explained. Frank set the basket on the table. "You're going to ask her out on a picnic."

"A picnic?"

"Yes," Elizabeth said. "A picnic."

Frank opened the basket. "We packed everything you need, even a blanket."

"You want me to take her on a picnic?"

She picked up the bag she had packed the night before. "There's plates, forks, a bottle of wine." She handed the bag over to him. "There's a pond through the woods that has a cute little sandy spot near a willow tree. I drew you a map."

Jack looked at the map dumbfounded. "A picnic?"

Elizabeth looked at Frank, disappointed. "This is how you woo a woman."

"I don't think Rachael is that kind of woman."

"Well, she isn't the kind who wants a guy to boss her around and tell her what she should do." She knew Jack meant well, but he also had the eldest-child-syndrome, where he wanted to fix things and did whatever it took to do so — his way. He didn't always understand that sometimes he didn't need to fix things for other people.

He picked up the bag. "Ask her on a picnic?"

"Ask her on a picnic," Frank and Elizabeth said in unison.

They watched as he backed away with the basket in one hand

and Elizabeth's bag in the other. As he threw it in his truck with Captain, Frank said, "It's as though he's never heard of Jane Austen."

Elizabeth nodded. "I don't think he's even watched a romantic comedy."

~

Jack pulled off the highway once he reached the Maine border into New Hampshire. Captain sat in the front seat, watching the road. He hit Route 4 and followed it up along the river before turning onto 106 to Profile Falls. The rolling hills soon turned into granite mountainside, and then he was alone on the road. The forest hugged the roadside and he slowed down along the curves, keeping a sharp eye out, with all the moose crossing signs posted every couple of miles.

After losing all signals, he shut off his radio, planning out what he was going to say when he saw her. Never in his life had he contemplated the process of asking a girl out as much as he did with Rachael. He'd just ask, and they usually said yes. Women seemed to want to hang on long after he wanted to move on, even when his brother married one of them.

Rachael completely threw him.

He liked women. He wasn't so into himself that he couldn't fall in love. He just didn't feel a need to have a serious relationship in his life yet. He always planned to, someday, he just never felt as though he'd met "the one".

The night he saw Rachael for the first time, something changed inside of him. Yes, she was beautiful. And yes, if he was honest with himself, he did enjoy the whole damsel-in-distress thing. He liked being able to help, but it was more than that. He would never admit this to his family, especially not Matt, but he felt something important that night. He was sure of it.

Now he just needed to convince her to take a chance and see how right they were together. He pulled onto another road before seeing the signs to Holly Lane Farm. As annoyed as he was with Elizabeth, he was glad she hooked Rachael up with a place to stay. Somewhere safe.

As he turned onto Holly Lane, he drove down through a wooden covered bridge, his tires making a low rumbling over the wooden boards. The road's windy path lead down to a farm nestled in the valley of the White Mountains. Row after row of pine trees lined the hillside.

His heart pounded as he pulled up the driveway. The gravel under his wheels announced his presence as he thundered up to the house. A woman with a baseball cap and cowboy boots walked out on the porch.

"You must be here for Rachael."

"Yes, I am, actually. She around?" He wrung his hands. "I'm Jack."

Maggie smiled, just like his mother did when he mentioned a girl's name. "Your sister called me, told me you were on your way, but I'm afraid you've missed her. She's run into town." Maggie looked at her watch. "She'll be back soon. In the meantime, you can come in and have a cup of coffee."

Disappointed, Jack faked a smile. "That sounds great."

Maggie had sent Rachael, in the farm truck, to town for all the weekly supplies. Rachael had never driven a truck before Finn's, which was a lot smaller, but her protests fell on deaf ears.

"You'll be fine," Maggie insisted as she handed over the keys. "Now, have you ever been to Profile Falls before?"

Rachael shook her head. "I've never been this far north before."

"Okay, well, if you turn right on that road up there." She pointed at the end of her road. "You'll hit Main Street and you'll find your way to the feed store, which is right where you pull into town."

The autumn colors blended together as she drove. Fall was everywhere, here, unlike in the city, where it came and went. Here color was everywhere, from the browning ferns to the purple asters with their orange centers. The last of the brown-eyed Susans stood tall, next to the pumpkins in Maggie's garden. A flock of geese formed a v and honked from above. Fall wasn't just about the trees, here. She could feel it all around her.

She rolled down her window, reading Maggie's hand-written directions every so often. When she stopped at the feed store, the owner loaded up the rear of the truck, almost filling the bed.

"You wouldn't happen to be the long-lost daughter, now would you?" he asked, a mischievous smile on his face.

"No, I'm afraid I'm not." Rachael wished it could be that simple. She'd gladly take the place of Maggie's daughter.

He clicked his tongue and shook his head. "Tell Maggie I'll charge her tab."

"Okay." Rachael pulled open the truck's door. "Thanks."

He nodded and headed back to the store.

Rachael racked up each new encounter as another witness. By the time she reached the bottom of the list, she forgot about the beautiful scenery surrounding her and the friendly people of Profile Falls. She just saw shadows and strangers, and she felt exposed.

She hurried toward home, her heart pounding as her anxiety grew. She wanted to get back to the farm, back where she could feel the fall, again.

As she pulled into the driveway, she saw a black truck sitting in front of the house. She stopped halfway up the driveway. Her heart dropped inside her chest. It wasn't until she saw the Maine plates that she realized who it was.

Jack.

Just as she thought his name, he stepped out the side door of Maggie's house and onto the porch. A smile grew across his face, and he waved. As she parked the truck, she left everything inside, and jumped out.

"What are you doing here?" She covered her smile with her hand. She wanted to be mad, but if she was honest with herself, she couldn't be happier.

His mouth opened just as she heard barking from around the corner. Four dogs ran around the barn, jumping and leaping onto each other, playing. Captain was right in the thick of it.

"Captain!" She knelt down and held out her arms. Captain ran from the group, his tongue hanging out, and jumped right into her, licking her face then falling to the ground, exposing his belly. "It's so good to see you."

Captain soon flipped over and ran to play with Maggie's dogs. Rachael stood up and faced Jack.

"What are you doing here?" she asked again. She wasn't upset, or nervous, or scared that someone had found her. She was relieved. And glad.

"Finn told me." He looked into her eyes, the green shades deepening the longer he stared at her under the autumn sun. "And I missed you."

"You missed me?" A laugh escaped. She couldn't believe he'd miss her. If anything, she figured he'd realize what a weight she was off his shoulders.

He stepped closer to her. "Plus, my sister told me I had to take you on a picnic."

"A picnic?" she laughed again, her nerves getting the best of her.

"I know just the spot." He pulled out a hand-drawn map.

She felt a rush of energy move all the way from her toes up her body. "That sounds lovely."

~

Jack laid the red and black checkered blanket down by the water's edge. The pond had a small sandy bank where the cattails and tall grass edged the border just like Elizabeth had drawn it.

Leaves floated on the water's surface among the lily pads. Elizabeth was right. It was the perfect spot.

"I can't believe you drove all the way up here." Rachael sat with her legs crossed, her knee almost touching his. He couldn't stop thinking of how badly he wanted to move closer.

"I couldn't stop thinking about you."

She smiled at his confession.

He passed over a sandwich, opening up the thermos to see what was inside. It smelled like minestrone. At the bottom of the basket was a tin, and he pulled off the top. "Mmm, they made apple strudel." He breathed in the aroma. "Plus, I wanted to have lunch with four dogs."

Rachael giggled as Captain and friends sat by the basket, waiting patiently for the first morsel of food to fall.

"I'm so glad you brought Captain. He looks great." She diverted her eyes from his, and looked down at her sandwich. "I suppose Elizabeth told you about why I left."

He shook his head. Loyalty had always been Elizabeth's strong suit. Plus, she enjoyed being secretive about everything, even the darn picnic. "I don't care about all that. All I care about is sitting right here by this pond, with you."

"Sounds perfect." She peeked in the basket. "What else did they pack?"

"Some more desserts and..." Jack held up the bottle. "And some wine."

He shook the homemade brownies. A Williams family recipe. He filled a bowl with minestrone and handed over a spoon.

As they ate, their conversation flowed naturally. Jack told her tales of being a kid in Camden Cove, and she told him about moving around. He made mental notes about her, and instead of asking further questions, waited for her to tell him more. She told him about her parents, and how her father left when she was a little girl. How she had heard that he lived in Florida. She didn't talk much about her mother, except to say that they didn't see eye to eye on a lot of things. She told him about how she lived with Finn as a child, and how she called him "Pops".

She never brought up any of her other relationships.

Off in the distance, moans from the sheep could be heard. He leaned back after he finished eating. "This place sure is nice."

There was a slight, sweet-smelling breeze. Jack snuck a peek at her.

"It really is." Her gaze set on the pond's still water.

Did she like it more here than Camden Cove?

She was about to say something, but stopped herself. There it was. The hesitation. He inventoried what he would have to pack up once she told him to get lost again.

"I can't…"

He let out a sigh. "It's cool, Rachael," he began. "I'm really here to check in, and make sure you're okay."

She picked at a piece of strudel. She then put it down and said, "I'm married."

Jack's heart pounded at her confession. "You're married?"

She blew out a breath, her shoulders fell. "Yes."

"Oh." He didn't know what to say, so he looked out at it, too. Married?

"I left him when I came to Camden Cove."

The image of her wet, rain-soaked body and black-and-blue eye flashed through his head. Adrenaline mixed with anger flooded every part of his body. Was the eye part of the reason why she left?

"I'm a mess you don't want to have deal with."

"What are you talking about?"

Rachael let out a breath and shook her head. "Believe me. You have no clue who I am."

"Come back to Camden Cove," he argued. "Stay in the apartment."

"I can't stay." She shook her head. "You don't understand."

"I can put an alarm on the door." Jack thought of other ways to make her feel safe. "I can put cameras in."

She shook her head. "You'd be better off forgetting about me."

"I've been miserable since you've left." He reached out for her hands, and she didn't pull away, but she didn't look at him.

"This is where I need to be for now."

"Are you positive someone was there in the apartment?" Jack understood why she'd be nervous, but there was no real sign of an intrusion.

She heaved a deep breath and then let it go. "No."

He nodded, but didn't say anything. Elizabeth's words filled his head. Let go. Suddenly, behind them, Captain and Maggie's dogs started wrestling each other and bounding into the water. Just as fast as they jumped in, they jumped back out and onto the blanket, all over their lunch.

"Captain, no!" Jack reached out, but missed Captain as he grabbed what was left of his sandwich as both bowls of soup tipped over.

Jack and Rachael raced to collect the rest of the food scattered across the blanket. The dogs ran back into the pond, playing and growling on top of one another.

Jack grabbed the corners of the blanket and pulled everything into the middle. Rachael followed and grabbed the other side, and he noticed a smile on her face. Soon, he heard her laughing as she collected the rest of the salad from the sand.

He almost argued one last time, to try to change her mind, but stopped himself. He looked at the dogs playing in the water and said, "Captain's not going to want to leave."

She bit her bottom lip. "Would you want to come back for another picnic?"

CHAPTER 14

*R*achael followed exactly what Fletcher did with the pines. The teenager showed her how to trim them by using a hand-held electric trimmer. As he walked around the orchard, he explained how to decipher the different types of trees that had been planted over the years. He showed her how he lined up the rows.

He removed his hat and wiped his forehead with his sleeve. "Tomorrow, if you have time, you can finish the last two rows."

"By myself?" She wasn't so sure. "What if I ruin them?"

He shook his head. "They always come back."

The rest of the day, Rachael followed Fletcher, asking questions about the farm, and he seemed to enjoy answering them. As they worked their way through a grove, Finn popped in her head and she wondered how he was doing on his own.

Everything seemed brighter, lighter. She knew it wasn't the fresh air or warm autumn sun. She hadn't felt like that since… ever. She laughed at the image of the dogs jumping in the water.

As the sun set behind the mountain, she sat out in an Adirondack chair underneath the large maple. Leaves dropping to the ground pitter-pattered all around her. Dark shadows lay upon the farm. Instinctively she turned toward the east, picturing the coast. Wondering what Jack might be looking at, at that very moment.

Then her stomach twisted. What was she doing? Jack didn't deserve someone like her. She hadn't even told him the whole truth. He doesn't know what she did. How could she be so selfish?

Maybe she was as selfish as Nick always said. Maybe she was a sorceress who played with people's emotions, not caring what pain she caused. She didn't want to hurt him, so why did she let him take her on that picnic? Why did she let him hold her hand, and make him think something was happening between them?

She wouldn't ever be able to be with him, because in order to really be able to give him everything, she'd have to give up everything. She'd have to come out of the shadows. She couldn't live on the run, waiting each day for someone to discover her secret. Or worse, have to keep moving forever, never getting anywhere. How could she ask that of him?

Yes, that was what Rachael feared.

He would.

Jack was the kind of guy who'd wait. And she couldn't live with herself if she let him.

Jack tapped his thumbs against the steering wheel as he drove into town. He turned up the music. The old classic he hadn't heard for years seemed to fit his mood, and he turned it up some more. The weather couldn't have been more perfect. Sun filtered through the colors, a late Indian summer hitting New England at the end of October. Pumpkins sat by doors, husks wrapped around door frames.

He wished Rachael had come back with him. He'd take her out. She couldn't be this close without seeing fall in Camden Cove. He was glad Stephen King wrote horror rather than romances, otherwise this picturesque scene would be flooded with even more tourists.

He recognized his mother's minivan as soon as he pulled into the parking lot. What was she doing there that early? He found her inside, behind her desk, her paper ledger of supplies opened. She didn't look up from her computer, her fingers typing in the order as efficiently as always. She could do her job while she slept.

"What's up, mom?" he asked as he stepped past her.

She pulled off her reading glasses. "I heard you went to see that woman, Rachael?"

He almost asked who told her, but with his family, it really didn't matter. "Yes, and I see you have something to say about it?" He eyed his mom. Forever nosy when it came to her children's personal lives, she didn't hold back her opinions.

"Do you really think it's a good idea?" she asked. "She seems to have a lot going on."

He was about to answer, when he stopped himself. Was he being selfish, pushing this relationship on Rachael? Had he done exactly what Elizabeth told him not to do?

"I like her."

Sarah stood up from the desk and gave him her look, lips pressed, eyebrows together, a slight tilt to her head. "The way she came into town makes me think there's a lot you don't know about her."

He nodded, crossing his arms. "Where are you going with this, mom?"

"I think you should be cautious."

"I think I'll be just fine." Jack stepped away from the conversation and toward his office. She had her own issues with new people in the Williams' inner circle, especially women who dated her sons. The line between her family and the rest of the world was clearly drawn. Her concern was real, he recognized, but there wasn't anything or anyone that could change his feelings for Rachael.

She followed him into his office. "Look, I know everyone's rooting for you two, and I'm not trying to get involved —"

"But?" he interrupted.

She gave him a look. "But honestly, she needs to find more help than what we can give her."

"What are you saying?"

"My point is, do you really know what's going on with her?"

Jack just looked at his mom. In many ways, she was crossing a line. A line he'd seen her cross before, and one he didn't appreciate. However annoyed and angry he was, he also couldn't argue with her. Rachael hadn't told him much. He really didn't know.

"Did you ever think there's more to the story than a black eye?" she spoke the words slowly.

He loved his mother and understood everything she said was out of concern, but his concern was for Rachael. "I know you mean well, but you raised me to protect the ones we care about."

He waited for her to respond to the words she had spoken a thousand times while he was growing up, but she restrained herself. She looked up at the ceiling and sighed.

"Didn't you teach us to stand up for the little guy, and take care of your neighbors?" He knew she would change her tune. He walked over to her and pulled her into a hug. Her kryptonite when it came to her kids.

"Yes, I did." She tucked herself closer against his chest. "Just be careful."

CHAPTER 15

aptain rode shotgun with Jack as he drove back to New Hampshire, driving the same winding roads to see Rachael. The fall colors had already dulled from the frost over the past few nights. The deep red shades had gone, leaving golden hues mingled with the greens of conifers along the mountains.

When his truck rolled up the gravel driveway, he saw Rachael walking out of the barn. The way she had her hair pulled back into a ponytail made her seem taller, stronger. A strong woman would leave a weak man — a controlling man. He admired how brave she was to do whatever it took to get away from his control, even if it meant running and sacrificing everything.

He squeezed the wheel as she stood there watching as he pulled up. She gave a little wave, but stood in the entrance of the barn. Maggie walked out from behind her and waved as well, a big smile on her face.

Captain started jumping around the truck to get out before Jack could even get his seatbelt off. "Hold on, Cap, let me help you out," he said, as Captain barked. His leg still made it difficult for him to jump down from the cab. When he got the dog out, he ran straight to Rachael.

She knelt and rubbed the dog's neck, giving him a big hug. Soon, a cacophony of barking came from the barn, and all three of Maggie's dogs came to greet their new friend. Captain left Rachael as soon as he saw them, jumping into the group.

"Welcome back," Maggie said as he got out of the truck, shaking his hand. She whistled for the dogs. "Let's go and get a treat!"

All four ran behind Maggie into the house.

"What are you doing here?" Rachael asked. She still hadn't moved from the barn.

"I couldn't wait to see you." He told the truth. No need to confuse things by trying to act nonchalant at this point. "And I like to shovel poop."

She smiled, her hand covering her mouth, but then made a face. "I have to work."

"I'm sure Maggie wouldn't mind the extra help." This time, he wasn't going to take no for an answer.

She tapped the wood floor of the barn with her boot heel a few times as she contemplated his offer. Her eyes slanted up toward him. "Alright, come along."

He struggled holding back his grin. He'd have to chill out. He didn't want to go and screw this up by pushing her. "What's first?"

She stuffed her hands in her pockets as she walked back inside the barn. "We need to muck out the stalls, then trim some trees."

She grabbed a couple of shovels and handed one over to him. "What about the restaurant?"

"I got someone to cover me."

Her lips widened, and this time she didn't cover it up.

"And what better way to spend my day than mucking out stalls?"

She laughed and walked over to the first stall. "Well then, you're in for a treat."

She opened the door and walked inside. Goats murmured as

she patted their heads while moving through the stall, then opened the outside gate. "There you go."

Jack had cleaned dozens of kitchens, but never had he cleaned up after farm animals. He looked around, trying to figure out what to do first.

"Want to grab the wheelbarrow?" Rachael asked, pointing at the wall behind Jack.

He grabbed the barrow and wheeled it to Rachael, who already had a shovel full of soiled straw. He followed her lead and filled the barrow. They hardly talked, but the quiet felt comfortable, like a blanket. Together, they worked in a steady rhythm. They shoveled up the straw along with the extras. When the barrow was full, he'd empty it in the field as Rachael filled the stall with fresh bedding.

He snuck glances at her throughout the morning, only catching hers a few times. For most of the day, Rachael had acted cool toward him. Had he mistaken what happened between them?

Why was she so hard to read?

She went to the wheelbarrow, now full, and started to grab the handles. He stepped over to help.

"I can get that." He watched as the wheelbarrow teetered from the weight of horse manure.

"I've got it."

He rubbed his forehead as he laughed.

"What?"

He picked up his shovel and shook his head. "You just cannot accept help."

"It's just that I can do it." She pushed the wheelbarrow over to the stall door, and the wheel stuck on a protruding edge of a floorboard. The barrow didn't move.

He stopped what he was doing and leaned against the shovel. "Would it really kill you to accept my help at this point?"

"I don't need your help."

"Everybody needs a little help, Rachael." He dropped the shovel against the wall. "Don't you trust me by now?"

~

"I don't trust anyone." She walked away, down to her favorite horse's stall. Pumpkin's chestnut coat shimmered under the sunlight. The horse stuck her head over the stall door, nudging Rachael's hands with her muzzle. His footsteps created a hollow beat against the floorboards.

"I see it this way," he said, leaning against the stall next to her. "I think you came into my restaurant that night for a reason, and that's so I could be there for you. You can't tell me that all those pieces fell perfectly into place by coincidence?"

She could smell his musky cologne, even a hint of the tangy scent of the sea.

"You can't help me," she said, her voice quivering.

"Maybe I'm here to be by your side?" He nudged her with his shoulder, smiling.

Her chest filled with air. She squeezed the railing of the stall.

"Come on, Rachael." He leaned closer and said, "You and me and Captain."

She looked down and there sat Captain, his tail wagging his whole body as he looked back and forth between them. Jack moved a bit closer, now bumping his hip into hers. He rested on his elbows. She could feel his breath against her cheek.

"I would really like to gain your trust."

He leaned closer but stopped just before his lips touched hers. Her chest rose up and down as he stood there, looking at her. All she could hear was her heartbeat in her ears as she waited for his next move. And without thinking anymore, she closed her eyes and pressed her lips to his. When she pulled back, they both took in a deep breath at the same time, staring at each other.

"I'm hoping this means I can stay for dinner." He gave her a sly smirk.

She rested her forehead on his chest. She couldn't believe this was happening.

He grabbed her hand and walked out of the barn, giving a whistle. "Come on, Cap! Let's eat!"

~

Rachael sat on the counter and watched as Jack started dinner.

"I can't believe you brought all this food." She said looking at all the containers.

"We cook a lot in my family," he said, rolling prosciutto around asparagus.

"What are you going to make us for dinner tonight?" she asked, as she pulled out a bag of flour.

"Pork tenderloin with apple chutney, and butternut squash ravioli in a caramel butter reduction." He winked at her. "I might be trying to impress you."

She pulled out fresh rosemary and thyme he had luckily found at a farm stand along the way. "You don't have to try to impress me."

He wanted to reach out and hold her, keep her in his arms forever, but instead he grabbed the bottle of wine, poured Rachael a glass, and began to do what Jack knew best. Cook.

"What can I do to help?" Rachael asked, leaning against the cabinet. Her knee touched his elbow, sending a current through his whole body.

She swung her hair behind her shoulders and a strand fell down in front of her eyes. He stopped chopping the rosemary and brushed the strand behind her ear. "Tell me more about you."

It looked like she was about to hesitate, but then said, "I grew up in Rhode Island after my dad left."

While she talked, the squash cooked, and he made the dough for the raviolis. He told her about going out on his grandfather's lobster boat, fishing with Matt and his cousins during the summers. She told him about life before her dad left, and how her mother continued to date the same kind of guy over and over again. He talked about how happy his parents were after thirty plus years of marriage.

He brought the plates over to the table Rachael had set earlier. He pulled out the chair for her as she sat down.

"Thank you."

"You're welcome." He lifted his glass to her. "To new beginnings."

"To new beginnings."

He took a sip and kept his eyes on her. "I've missed you like crazy." He stopped and put his drink down. "I know that sounds crazy. I hear how crazy I sound, but I couldn't stop thinking about you."

He shook his head as the only sound was of a lone cricket could be heard. The mood changing.

"Jack… It's just…"

"What?" It was her time to confess. Had he not proved he could be trusted? But as they sat there, she didn't speak. "Talk to me, Rachael."

Her eyes watered and she immediately looked away.

"What if I told you something that I've never told anyone, and then you tell me something?"

She gave him a weary look. "Okay."

Jack rubbed his hands together and then said. "I've only been in love once before."

"I'm not sure if that's much of a confession."

"With my brother's wife." He waited for it to register and then her expression changed.

"The woman above the restaurant?"

He nodded. "I had been in love with her since I was a kid, actually, but when I left for school, she broke it off. When I came back, she and my brother had started dating, and then, well, the rest is history."

He hadn't told anyone his confession and the way her eyes widened, his vulnerability rose.

"Wow."

"Yup." He took a long drink of wine.

He thought of Justine running out of the apartment, pleading with him. Her feet bare. Her shirt misbuttoned. Had she slept with Freddy above the restaurant, to get back at Matt or Jack?

"Do you still love her?"

He shook his head. "No. Now I feel sad for her."

"Strange, how you could fall in love with someone who turns out so wrong for you."

❦

It was her turn. Her flight response triggers started up immediately. Her breathing became shallow, hard to control. Her hands trembled, even pressed under her legs. Her stomach seemed to press against her throat.

Jack waited.

She looked at him, praying he'd understand. "I never told anyone he hit me. My mom knew, but we never talked about his abuse. I had been planning to leave, hiding money, sneaking stuff out of the house so when the time came, I'd be ready to leave, but he must've found out." A tear dropped from her eye and Jack wiped it away. "I was making a cup of tea at the stove. Then I heard this click and felt the cold steel of his gun on the back of my head. He told me that was a warning, and to tell him what I had been planning. That's when he hit me in the face." Her hand instinctively went to her eye. She stopped, trying to think of the words, trying to think of a way to explain. Her breath steadied as tears suddenly stung her eyes. The image of the moment she was about to describe was as clear as the day she lived it. "I fell against the stove, and I grabbed the first thing my hands touched and swung. I screamed so loud, I didn't hear his body fall onto the floor… but when I opened my eyes, and he was laying there, I knew I had to go. That's when I left."

Jack didn't say anything, just listened.

"I ran to my mom's place, where I'd hidden everything." She could still see her mom standing in her bathrobe, begging her to go back to see if he was okay. "I got on the bus and went as far as I could afford to go. I should've checked to see if he was okay."

He looked straight into her eyes. "You had no other choice. He could've killed you."

She felt a nudge on her leg, and Captain barked. They both looked down. Captain suddenly jumped up on the two of them, licking Jack's face.

"Ugh, come on, Cap," Jack said, wiping off the slobber. "That's not helping."

Rachael's anxiety loosened as she watched the two interact. As Jack tried to get Captain to settle down, it only riled him up even more. The dog ran in circles, barking.

"How about a walk?" he asked, but directed the question at her.

"A walk, at night?"

"How else do you see the stars and listen for owls?"

He held out his hand, waiting. She didn't take it, just looked at it, not sure.

"Take it, Rachael," he whispered to her. "Trust me."

She reached out, her fingers fitting perfectly into his.

CHAPTER 16

*J*ack awoke to Captain licking his face. He sat beside the couch where Jack slept. As the dog's tail banged against the coffee table, he moaned low in his throat. That little bugger had woken him up. With one eye, Jack peeked at his watch, the sky still as dark as night.

"Cap," Jack whispered. "It's still early. Lay down."

He closed his eye again and shifted on the couch. He listened for Rachael. He didn't hear anything except another set of low moans coming from Captain.

Jack let out a hushed huff and sat up. Rachael's door was still open, the light on beside her bed. She lay on her side, facing away from him. She laid still. He grabbed his sweatshirt and tiptoed over to the door. Captain jumped up, looking out. When he opened it up, the dog ran straight to the grass, sniffing around. He definitely had some hound in him.

All the downstairs lights in Maggie's house had been turned on. The smell of bacon drifted out from inside. The morning was quiet, not a sound besides Captain sniffing around in the bushes. From the east, below the tree line, a soft orange and pink glow rose up. The farm emerged slowly from the night's shadows. As beautiful as it was, he wished he could hear the familiar rhythm of the ocean's pulse. The waxing and waning of the water against the rocky coast helped him think, take things in, because his thoughts were wild and out of control.

He understood everything from this point forward would be up to Rachael, but he hoped she'd trust him enough to be open to some of his ideas. There were no reports of a police officer being hurt in the news. No notice of a missing woman from Rhode Island. Nothing about such a crime, or about Rachael, anywhere, at least not on Google.

He thought back to when he went to visit his buddy Alex, hoping he had forgotten about his request to look into Rachael. Alex hadn't mentioned anything, but Jack knew his friend well enough to know he wouldn't forget. Now he had to figure out if he should tell Rachael what he asked Alex to do, and risk freaking her out, or talk to Alex first. He might've been busy with the storm. He might not have looked into anything yet. He pulled out his phone.

Don't worry about that favor.

Alex responded right away. **No?**

Jack responded casually back. **All good.**

He decided for now, he'd keep this to himself. No need to get Rachael upset for nothing.

Rachael started a pot of coffee and watched as Jack ran around in the pasture with Captain, throwing a stick. She smiled as the two played. A bond had developed between them already. She poured a cup for Jack and walked with it out onto the porch.

"Morning." Her breath billowed out as she walked down the steps, the grass stiff from frost.

"Good morning." His smile made his eyes glow in the morning rays.

Jack had been a complete gentleman the whole night. He didn't pressure her into telling more of her story, although she did anyway. When he slept on the couch, he didn't question why she slept with the lights on. She fell asleep as soon as her head hit the pillow feeling safer than she ever had. She hadn't slept that deeply in years.

"Did you sleep well?" he asked as she passed the cup of coffee to him, steam rising from the cup.

"Perfect." She couldn't keep her eyes off him in the morning sun. Something about his brown stubble and messed up hair made him even more attractive.

He breathed in, and moved closer to her. "You should come back with me today. Finn would love to see you."

"I can't." She shook her head. "Maggie's going to be in the barn soon, doing the morning chores."

Jack pulled out his phone and texted. Sliding it back in his pocket, he said, "I guess I'll have to stay here with you."

Rachael smiled, but gave him a look. "But what about the restaurant?"

"My mom and dad would love to run things, believe me."

She looked over at Maggie's house, then back to him. "That would be perfect." She leaned forward to kiss him, but startled by the sound of a screen door slamming. All three dogs came charging at them. Captain took off towards them, and she and Jack were smack dab in the middle of their reunion.

"Morning!" Maggie called from the porch. "Anybody want breakfast?"

Rachael bit her bottom lip as she looked at Jack. He kissed her cheek quickly, then waved at Maggie. "I smell bacon."

He ushered Rachael out of the mob of dogs by placing his hand on the small of her back. His touch was gentle, but she could feel her body heating where he rested his hand.

He opened the door for her as they reached the porch. Maggie gestured at the full table. Pancakes, scrambled eggs, bacon, and sausage. A glass bottle of maple syrup sat next to bottles of ketchup and tabasco sauce.

"You didn't forget a thing," Jack said, pulling out a chair for Rachael.

"It's nice to be able to cook for someone." Maggie pushed the plates closer to them. "Well, dig in."

"Are you staying for the Pumpkin Festival?" Maggie asked, as they filled their plates.

"There's a festival?" Jack spooned eggs onto his plate, then looked at Rachael. "That sounds fun."

"You have to go if you're in town. Thousands of pumpkins lit up along the streets. Half of them are mine!" Maggie paused and said, "Do you mind if I say grace?"

"Not at all." Rachael put her napkin in her lap and Jack took her hand. Her heart skipped a beat at his gesture, almost leaping out of her chest. She instinctively started to cover her smile, but he squeezed her hand, holding on.

"Thank you Lord, for blessing us with this beautiful morning together with this bountiful food. Thank you for bringing Rachael here to help on the farm along with her friend, Jack. May you bless them with good health and love, always. Amen."

"Amen," Jack said back, but held onto her hand, until Maggie asked him to serve the pancakes.

Rachael could still feel his touch as she placed her hands in her lap, tears stinging the back of her eyes. She didn't want to look up, because she was sure she'd start crying. She'd never been happier in her life. Her emotions spilled over.

"Rachael?" Jack said, as a tear fell into her lap. "You okay?"

Rachael sniffled and nodded, using her other hand to wipe it away. "I've never been better."

∾

Jack spent the whole day following Rachael around the farm, feeding animals, trimming trees. They loaded pumpkins in Maggie's truck for an emergency delivery to the festival.

"They're about to break the record!" Maggie sped out of the driveway.

By the afternoon, when the sun started to settle in the distance, Jack stopped her in the middle of the barn and kissed her, like he had all day between chores. Whenever there was a free moment or time to spare, he'd kiss her, breathe in her scent, take in everything about her before he had to let her go and get back to work. "You still want to head into town?"

She stopped shoveling, holding onto its handle. "I don't know."

"Come on," he said, wrapping his arms around her waist. "I'll get you some cotton candy."

But he could see her worry working like a disease spreading through her blood. The longer she hesitated, the more he worried for her. Living a life of fear would be just as isolating as her life before, with Nick.

"I'll be there with you," he said. He could see her sinking further in. He took hold of her hand and squeezed it.

"Okay." But she looked uneasy about it.

Unable to hold back, he kissed her again, and when they finally parted, he said, "We should probably help with the record."

"Huh?"

He pulled her out of the barn by the hand, picking up a pumpkin from the patch. "We should carve Captain."

He heard her laugh, and felt that warm feeling inside his chest. He gave a loud whistle. All the dogs came barreling through the barn door. Barking enveloped them as the dogs bounced around each other.

"Let's go, Cap," he commanded, and Captain left the group, following at Jack's heels. He stopped and kissed her one last time before they went back in. He wanted to keep Rachael as happy as she had been all day. Show her what life could be like together.

After carving what ended up being a ghost instead of a dog, they headed to the festival with Captain. Her lips and her taste lingered on his mind as they drove. Turning the music's volume up, he played a country song he had never appreciated until that moment about how love could change a man's life. Never had lyrics spoken to him more than they did at that moment. Sneaking a glance at her, he almost told her how he felt, but for some reason hesitated.

By the time they reached the little town of Profile Falls, the sun had fallen behind the houses. Thousands of glowing jack-o-lanterns lined the main street. After they registered their pumpkin, Jack and Rachael walked hand in hand as they looked at all the different kinds of carvings. Some stuck to a Halloween theme with cats and witches and scary faces, while others had cool designs or words.

"Look!" Rachael pointed to a row of pumpkins that spelled out 'Will you marry me?' "That's so sweet."

Under a tent, they saw Maggie with some of her friends at the pig roast, and joined them for dinner. Every time Jack noticed Rachael's body tense up or stiffen, he'd make sure she remembered he was close, either by holding her hand, or giving her a light touch. Something to remind her she wasn't alone.

After they ate, they sat around talking as the band set up.

"You two dance?" Maggie asked.

Rachael looked out as people cleared the tables and chairs away from the dance floor. "I loved to go dancing."

Jack took that as an invitation, and as soon as the music began, he handed over Captain's leash to Maggie, grabbed Rachael's hand, and tugged her toward the tiny open space in front of the stage. Placing one hand on the small of her back, he took her other hand in his. She stood back, slightly unsure, but he drew her in closer, moving in sync to the rhythm of the music. Soon she fell into step with his lead.

"You can really dance," she said impressed.

"My grandmother taught us kids when we spent the night at

her house. Elizabeth was always my partner." That made her laugh. He moved her around the dance floor with only a simple two-step. "This is about all I know."

"It's perfect." She gave him a look before resting her head against his shoulder. He wanted this moment to last forever. He made a silent promise that he'd never let anyone hurt Rachael again. He'd do whatever he had to do in order to protect her.

CHAPTER 17

*J*ack watched as Rachael slept in the crook of his arm on the couch as an old DVD played. He had lost the feeling in his arm at least an hour ago, but he hadn't moved for fear of waking her up. She actually looked serene, calm. Every time she stirred, he would lean into her movements.

When the movie credits rolled, Jack shifted and shoved his arm underneath her legs, and in one movement he swept her up. Her eyes shot open and she jumped out of his arms, back onto the couch.

"Whoa!" He held out his hands as Rachael caught her breath. "I'm sorry. You fell asleep and I was going to carry you to your bed."

Her eyes were wide with alarm. "I didn't realize I fell asleep."

Captain stretched as he got up from the floor. "I'll bring Cap outside one last time. I can close everything up when I come back in."

"You're staying here, right?"

He nodded.

He kissed her on the forehead. "I'll be right back."

He opened the door and let Captain out before he gave away his disappointment. Not that he wanted things to move quickly, but he still didn't know her feelings. His breath steamed under the porch light. He stepped down onto the grass and looked up to the night sky. The stars felt closer that night than most.

The night air had a bite to it, and he wished he'd grabbed his coat before going out. Captain sniffed along the back of the barn. The night's silence made him think too much. He knew Adam would be able to help her. He didn't know the law, but she had a reason to protect herself. If her husband had been hurt or worse, he was sure there would have been news about it. Nick wasn't on that floor anymore, that was for sure.

It took all he had not to go after Nick himself.

"Hurry up, Cap," he whispered as the dog moseyed around, finding the perfect spot.

Rachael was already in bed, when he came in from outside, her back to him with the bedside lamp on. He quietly took off his boots and walked toward the couch, which had a pillow and a couple of blankets on it. He sat down, looking at her. Captain moaned as he stretched out on the floor in front of her bed.

He let out a long sigh as he leaned back on the couch and fell asleep.

Before he knew it, he woke to a rooster crowing. Outside, gray clouds covered the sky, but enough light illuminated the windows to give the small cabin's interior a warm glow. Jack noticed that Rachael wasn't in the bedroom. He looked around. The bathroom door was open, but the room was empty. He looked outside and saw the lights on in the barn, and Maggie's house fully aglow.

Stretching as he sat up, he grabbed his shirt before heading to the door. Cold air rushed into the cabin, and he stepped outside quickly. Rubbing his hands to fight the chill, he walked to the barn.

As he passed by Maggie's place, Captain ran out of the barn and straight at him. Barking ensued from inside the house. The kitchen door opened and Maggie's dogs came charging out.

"Morning!" Maggie waved from the door.

"Morning," he said back.

"How'd you sleep?" her tone was mischievous.

"Fine." Not wanting Maggie to get the wrong impression he added, "The couch is really comfortable."

She chuckled. "I'm glad to hear it." She waved again as she closed the kitchen door.

As he rounded the corner into the barn, he stopped as he saw Rachael rubbing the horse's neck, talking to it. The calm and serene Rachael, not the frightened, wild-eyed woman of last night.

"Hey," he said, walking up to her.

"I thought I'd let you sleep." She continued to pet the horse.

He dreaded what he was about to say. "I'm going to head back, probably soon."

She nodded, stepping slightly away from him… or was he just overthinking? She rubbed the horse's back.

He followed her. "I was thinking I could come back in a couple days."

She smiled, but kept her eyes on the horse, stepping a bit further back. She scratched on the horse's thigh. "Okay."

He tugged at her hand and catching her eyes. "You okay?"

Her forehead creased. "I don't want you to feel you have to come back."

He made a face at her. "I want to come back."

Her focus went back to the horse, but he noticed tears clinging to the corners of her eyes.

"What's going on, Rachael?" He moved closer to her. "Talk to me."

She faked a smile. "I'm fine."

"I'll be back here in a couple of days," he reassured her.

"Yup," she took in a breath, then blew it out.

"Or you could just come back with me, right now."

She shook her head. "A couple days?"

He tried to catch her eyes again, but she kept shifting them away before he could really see what was going on. But something had changed with Rachael between last night and this morning.

~

Something in the pit of Rachael's stomach told her to tell him to stay, but instead she shook her head as he got ready to leave.

"Come back with me," Jack pleaded as they walked to his truck. It had been at least his fifth time trying to convince her.

She wanted so badly to say yes. It would be so easy. Jack would take care of her. She knew he was one of the good guys. She'd be unbelievably happy, but would he?

She took a step back toward the barn. "I can't."

She thought of the night before. Jack a complete gentleman, sleeping on the couch, not pushing her boundaries. It hadn't been easy to lie in her bed, alone, knowing he was only feet away from her. She could feel the heat coming off him even from the other room.

And now he was asking her to come back with him. How come life threw her everything she wanted when she couldn't have it?

"Jack, please." She didn't want to argue.

"Think about coming back, though. After some time. Come back and start a new life, a better one, with me."

CHAPTER 18

*R*achael soon fell into a routine at the farm. Even though she set an alarm each night, she always woke before it went off. She enjoyed her mornings on the farm and looked forward to being in the barn with the animals, watching the sun creep over the mountains. But no matter how beautiful the scenery, her thoughts were far away.

Adam kept her in the loop with all the divorce proceedings. He had motioned for her information to be kept confidential. From what Adam could tell, Nick had been cooperating, but she still didn't trust him.

Maggie handed Rachael an envelope as Rachael brought in horses from the pasture. "Well, this is for the last two weeks."

Rachael looked at the cash inside. "This is way too much."

"Nonsense, you earned it, working as much as you have." Maggie removed her baseball cap and wiped her forehead with her arm. "Tomorrow's Sunday, and I'm insisting you take a day off."

"What about you?"

"I'll be fine." Maggie threw her hat back on. "Now go get that Jack Williams. You deserve yourself some happiness."

Rachael knew exactly what she wanted to do. The phone rang a few times before Finn answered.

"You coming for dinner?" he asked.

"I was hoping to take you out to eat."

He huffed. "Don't need to go and spend your money on me."

"Well, I want to." She didn't care what he was going to say, she wanted to do this. "I would like to take you to The Fish Market."

"With those overpriced meals!"

"Finn."

"Pops!" he huffed into the receiver. "If you make me put on a tie, then you're going to call me Pops."

"Okay." The idea of calling him *Pops* made her happy. "I'll see you tomorrow, Pops."

He grumbled something before hanging up.

All night, she contemplated calling Jack, telling him she would be in town, but didn't. Something inside told her not to get his hopes up, but really it was her hopes she didn't want to dash. Instead, she lay awake, imagining walking the trail with him and Captain, before finally falling asleep.

The next morning, she didn't waste much time getting ready. She tidied up the cabin by putting all of her things into her backpack, and took her savings out of the tin coffee can in the freezer. She planned to pay Finn for his truck, whether he wanted the money or not. She looked around the small cabin before she closed the door. It was as if she had never even been there.

On the way through Profile Falls, she past a small dress shop, where she'd noticed a burgundy dress in the window that would be perfect for dinner. She swung the truck against the sidewalk and bought it without even trying it on.

Before she knew it, she pulled the truck into Finn's driveway. He stepped out onto the porch as soon as she parked. She noticed that he had put out bright yellow mums on his doorstep.

"You hit any traffic?" he asked, as though the backroads of New Hampshire and Maine had regular traffic jams.

"Nope, no traffic at all." She grabbed her bag from inside the cab, not really sure why she'd brought her belongings.

She walked up the front steps and followed Finn inside. The house had been cleaned and things didn't appear as dull as before. The tabletops had been dusted and the curtains opened.

"I made a reservation for about an hour from now," he said. "I figured we didn't want to take our chances, with all the leaf-peepers clogging up the town."

"That sounds good." She pointed to the bathroom. "Do you mind if I change?"

"You can use your mom's room, upstairs. It's got its own washroom."

"Thanks," she said, twisting the string of her bag.

She ducked her head as she climbed the stairs, afraid to hit the low ceiling. The whole second floor was one long, skinny room. The single dormer held a window seat. She peeked out and could just make out the harbor. Shelves lined one half of the wall with boxes, books, and baskets full of things she imagined had been stored up there for years. But the place looked picked up, and the bed freshly made.

She walked over to a bulletin board with memorabilia tacked to it. Rubbing her thumb on the push pins, she pulled off a photograph. It was of her mother as a teenager, standing with a group of girls. She looked so happy and carefree. Rachael hadn't seen that side of her mother for so many years. She stuck the pin back into its original hole.

Had she known what the future held would she do it all again?

She may be frightened Nick might find her, but as she looked at her mother's familiar eyes, she was more afraid she'd be like her mother and go back to him.

～

Jack walked from the kitchen into the lobby to check on the numbers. Apparently, leaving town without telling people got some of the townsfolk curious — and hungry. The Fish Market was swamped. There were the usual tourists, but for a Sunday night, more locals came out for dinner than they'd had in years.

"Everything going okay with the restaurant?" Steve Gendron, the mayor, asked.

Jack shouldn't have been surprised at how quickly something as insignificant as taking a day or two off from work could escalate. "Everything's fine, Steve, just took a day for myself."

"A couple of days, I heard."

He eyed Jack, waiting for more information, but Jack ignored the nosy man. He decided to sit the mayor and his wife at the table against the windows. It was the furthest spot from the kitchen, so he wouldn't have to have any further interaction. Walking back to the kitchen, he checked the line. Order slips hung on the rack. Two cooks worked the line, and another on prep.

"Two out on lobster!" Michael, his sous chef, called out, just as Sandra, his best server, walked in from the floor.

"You'd never believe who just showed up with Finn McCabe."

Jack immediately checked out the floor, but couldn't see her. "Who?"

"The woman who lived above the restaurant. Pretty good for an old timer." Sandra stuffed another slip on the rack and started pooling her plates together, checking the dishes. "They're at table twelve."

Jack helped with her order and followed her out to the floor. The table sat close to the windows, but near the fireplace. A perfect two-person table that he usually gave to couples. He saw Finn first. Rachael's back was toward him, but then she looked over and smiled.

He lost his breath. She had always looked beautiful, but tonight she looked stunning in a burgundy dress. She wore makeup, with her hair hanging loose below her shoulders. She also appeared completely content. Happy, even.

He walked right up to their table, resting his hand on the back of Finn's chair, but kept his eyes on Rachael, wishing they were the only two people in the room. "You look beautiful."

"Doesn't she?" Even Finn looked happy, and Jack had never seen the old man smile.

"Thank you." Rachael tucked her hair behind her ears. Was she blushing?

The floor was almost full, and half the room seemed to be watching them. He suddenly wanted everyone to know Rachael, for her to be part of this town and part of his family and friends. He wanted her to be part of his life.

Sandra walked up with her pad in her hand.

"How's it going, Finn?" she asked.

Jack expected his usual gruff answer, but instead, Finn said, "Sandra, have you met my granddaughter, Rachael?"

"Oh, your granddaughter!" Sandra appeared as surprised as Jack was when he heard. She pointed at Rachael. "Yeah, I think I've seen you around."

Jack waited as Sandra took their order, even though he noticed a table waving for his attention. He couldn't take his eyes off her, wondering what she'd like from the menu.

"I'll have the roasted chicken."

All three gave Rachael a look. Sandra didn't write it down, as though she didn't believe her. "You want the chicken?"

"Don't you like seafood?" Finn asked.

Sandra shook her head. "Get the lobster pie. It's our fall special, and I promise you won't regret it."

"We'll both take it, with the steamed mussels as an app." Finn closed up his menu. "Might as well see what everyone talks about."

Jack took the menus and said, "I didn't know you were coming to town."

"She's having Sunday dinner with her grandfather." Finn pointed across the room. "Is that the mayor?"

"Apparently taking a day off from the restaurant is news that spreads fast."

Rachael looked around the room. "Why are they all looking at us?"

Sandra stuffed her pad into her apron and said, "Because it appears that Jack Williams is off the market."

~

When Rachael and Finn arrived back at his place, he convinced her to come inside for a cup of coffee. "It'll help with the drive home."

She got out and followed him into the house, wondering what it was like for him to live here all alone, for all those years. She had never met her grandmother, who had died shortly after Rachael was born. That was another point of contention between her, Finn, and her mother. Finn had blamed her grandmother's poor health on her mother leaving.

She wondered if Finn had been like her own father, as she watched him spoon the coffee grinds into the filter. He certainly was an angry old man, but with a good heart, that she was sure of. With all the troubles her mother put her grandparents through, she never mentioned him losing control, besides losing control over her.

"Wish you could help at the tavern." He turned the coffee maker on. "You had a real nice system going before you left. I'm afraid that I've already messed it up."

He gathered a pair of mugs and poured the coffee once it was ready. Steam rose from her cup as he placed it in front of her and sat down at his spot. As she blew on her coffee, she looked around, taking in all the little knickknacks and tchotchkes. She remembered the spoon and fork hanging on the wall from her stay as a little girl.

"So, next Sunday, pot roast?" he asked.

She nodded, so many things rolling inside her head, like a tidal wave spinning out of control. "Bring something green?"

Finn nodded.

There was so much she wanted to say, but instead she just slipped the envelope toward him.

"What's this?" He held it up.

"It's for the truck."

He tossed it back at her. "You don't have to pay me for that piece of junk."

Even with the high mileage, Finn took good care of the truck. "It's hardly junk."

Finn thumped his mug on the table. "I won't take it."

She shifted uncomfortably in her seat at his outburst. "Okay, but I don't want to be some charity case. I'd like to pay for what I take."

"I don't give to charities!" he huffed. "You're family. Now, you better get going before it gets too late."

His outburst startled her, but his face didn't look upset, instead a bit sorrowful. Setting her coffee down on the table, she stood up and said, "Well, then you're going to have to let me bring more than just greens for Sunday dinner."

She thought she saw the corner of Finn's mouth rise, just before he grabbed her mug and shooed her out the door.

"Don't stop at any of those rest stations to get gas, neither."

Finn stood under the porch light until she pulled out of the driveway and turned the corner, heading out of town. As she drove down Main Street, she strained her neck, looking down Harbor Lane, trying to get one last look at the restaurant. Then, without thinking, she pulled a U-turn and headed back, swinging into the parking lot faster than she intended. As she parked, she looked for his truck, but didn't see it. Then she saw the waitress who had served her, coming out the door.

"Hey, is Jack still there?" she asked.

The woman shook her head. "No, he left a while ago."

Jack got the call right after Finn and Rachael left. His buddy Billy called from Finn's to tell him about Justine.

"She needs someone to take her home."

"Did she show up with Freddy?" What was Justine doing, drinking at a bar by herself?

"Nope, just her."

Jack walked into the tavern about ten minutes later to see Justine leaning over a table with an older guy and his buddies. She had always been a flirt when she drank, but this was beyond that.

"Well, if it isn't Jack Williams." Her words slurred as she stood up, gripping the table's edge for support.

"Let me take you home, Justine." He looked at the small crowd watching them.

"Isn't that the way? Jack Williams, here to swoop in and save the day." She walked away from him, flinging her hand in his face. He reached out as she stumbled, but she ripped her arm out of his grip. "I don't need you!"

"Come on, Justine, let me take you home."

Tears fell down her face. "It's always been you, Jack," she slurred. "It's always been you."

He never expected her to say it, especially out loud in front of others. It had been something he had always secretly wanted, but now he wanted nothing more than to get Justine out of their lives forever.

She slumped into a chair and flung her head on her arm, her shoulders shaking as she sobbed in front of the crowd.

"I should bring you home." He pulled her up and steered her toward the door before she could say more.

"You broke my heart." She started talking louder as she walked through the crowd. "You just let me marry Matt. You didn't even care."

He ignored her ranting as she continued to twist the past.

Once outside the tavern, he opened the door to his truck and got her inside. He could hear her yelling at him through the window. When he got inside, she was crying into her hands. "I never stopped loving you, ever."

He didn't speak the whole drive home as she wailed out her cries. She cried with her whole body. As he slowed down in front of her house, she leaned over and tried to kiss him, but he moved away, slipping out of the truck. He opened the door for her and she wiped her eyes as she walked up to the door. She fished in her purse, grabbing her keys, stumbling on her feet.

After a third attempt to unlock the door, he grabbed the keys and opened the door, holding her elbow as she stepped up into the house.

"You going to be okay?" he asked, but felt sorry for her either way.

Instead of answering, she slammed the door in his face.

As he drove home, he held out hope that Rachael would still be at Finn's, but when the truck was missing, he wasn't surprised when Finn told him she had left. "Sorry, son, she left just a few minutes ago."

When he got home, Captain poked his head up from his usual spot on the couch in front of the window. He jumped off the couch as soon as he turned off the engine. He could hear his howls all the way inside the truck.

Just as he stepped inside and was about to turn on the lights, a flash of headlights hit the living room wall. Could it be?

When he opened the front door, she was almost at the steps, then stopped where she was. "I was wondering if that apartment was still available?"

He opened the door wide, pulling her into his arms and kissing her.

CHAPTER 19

*J*ack walked up to the boat slip holding two beers. He planned out exactly how he was going to break the news to Matt. He needed the apartment back. It was that simple. Rachael wanted to have her own place. Since he technically owned the building and was the landlord of the apartment, he had the right to lease it to anyone. And he had told Rachael it was available.

"Are you kidding me?" Matt leaned against the railing of his boat. He crossed his arms, snatching the beer out of Jack's hand. Seagulls swooped around them, searching for morsels and diving in the Atlantic wind.

"Come on, you know you can stay at my place as long as you want." Jack decided to make the offer even sweeter. "Rent free."

"How can you kick your brother out again?" Matt shook his head. "Where am I supposed to go now?"

"You're not a destitute." Jack understood that taking the apartment away from Matt, again, wasn't convenient for him, but Rachael needed the apartment more than he did. Matt couldn't argue that. "If you don't want to stay with me, you could stay with mom and dad. Or at Elizabeth's old place."

"They have Michelle staying there, when she visits Lucy."

Matt cracked open the beer and gave him a dirty look. "You owe me."

"I'll make it up to you, I promise."

"My laundry."

"Your what?" Jack twisted the cap off his own beer.

"I want someone to do my laundry, tidy my fishing gear, clean up my room, I'd like to have meals."

"You're not doing me the favor here." Jack couldn't believe Matt's nerve. "Even mom will be with me on this one."

Matt shrugged. "Laundry and dinner."

"Seriously?" Jack stood straighter and gave his brother a look. He took another sip, contemplating whether he should shove Matt overboard. "Fine."

"So, you're tangled up in this, now?" He knew that Matt's question was rhetorical, but he didn't want Matt to get a bad feeling about this.

"I like her."

Matt let out a deep breath. "When do I have to move out?"

"Now." Jack made a face, then patted his brother on the arm.

"Seriously?" Matt downed the beer.

"I'll get your laundry done."

Matt handed him his empty and took Jack's beer out of his hand. "You're literally kicking your brother onto the street."

"Into a top-of-the-line, queen size bed."

Jack did feel bad. "I know all this is really bad timing."

"Really bad."

"But I won't give you a hard time, if you want to try to work on your marriage. I won't get in the way."

"There's no marriage." Matt blew out. "Too much has happened for it to ever be good again."

"I'm sorry about everything between you and Justine." Jack meant it. He never wanted his brother hurt.

Matt took another drink and nodded, then said, "So this is the real deal then?"

Jack wished he had brought more beer. "Yeah, it's real."

Rachael tried to get used to her strange new normal, which seemed to include everyone in the small town. On most days, she and Jack spent the day together before he worked at the restaurant and she at the tavern.

Jack had practically moved into the apartment. Rachael insisted she'd be okay without him staying, but she liked him there. She felt safer with him there. As the weeks passed and fall blended into winter, she became less worried and anxious about being alone. She just missed not being around him.

In the mornings, he'd come over for coffee, and then they'd walked Captain along the Coastal Trail. Captain would run ahead as they walked behind together, enjoying the morning sunrise. They'd walk all the way to Perkin's beach. His hand always holding onto hers.

"This is the local beach," Jack explained as they stood watching the waves lap up against the shore. Wind blew her hair across her face, and he wiped the loose strands away with his fingertips. She imagined what it would be like in the summer, with colorful umbrellas dotting the sand and children running into the water. She liked being a local.

She grabbed his hand and squeezed. "I love you, Jack."

He smiled, leaning into her. "I love you, too."

They kissed as Captain ran into the water, chasing the waves up and down the sand. He swept her up into a hug, holding her so close she could feel his heartbeat. Then, without warning, he picked her up, off of her feet and into his arms.

Her eyes widened as he ran toward the water. "What are you doing?!"

"It's called the penguin plunge. It's the local rite of passage." He ran faster as he headed toward the water with Captain galloping happily behind them. Her arms squeezed around his neck so tight, she was sure she was choking him, but he laughed and kissed her again, only hitting the edge of the water. "You only get one save."

He set her gently down on her feet, waiting until the wave had retreated.

"You're lucky I like you." He laced his fingers into hers and pulled her along.

Above them, seagulls sang out, reminding her of how free she felt. How happy she was with Jack, and living in this town, seeing Finn every day.

"As a little girl, I used to wish I could fly with the seagulls." She had never told anyone of her silly little daydreams, suddenly feeling childish at her confession. A lone seagull flew down in front of them. "To be free, like them."

They stood watching the seagull dip down near the water and rise back up again into the wind. He wrapped his arm around her and pulled her close to him as the seagull flew off into the blue sky, crossing the beach and flying above the granite cliffs. He stood behind her as they faced the water and whispered, "You're free now, Rachael."

And for the first time, she believed him.

When they returned from the beach, Jack let go of her hand. "I've got to go and make some phone calls, but I'll make lunch and be up in a little bit." Jack handed Captain's leash to her and kissed her.

"I can come down and help with the supply orders." She had enjoyed helping at the restaurant, being with Jack in his element. One of her favorite things was watching him in the kitchen. He'd give her that look of his, making her feel crazy for him.

"Don't worry about it. I'll be up in a bit. What do you say to going for a drive out to the farm to see Maggie?"

"You want to take a day off?" Rachael was surprised. Even though she hadn't been back for long, she understood why the whole town was concerned Jack had taken time off when he stayed at the farm. Jack never took time off, especially not a whole day for a drive.

"I can live on the edge."

The seriousness of his tone contrasting with the playfulness in his eyes, made her laugh. "That sounds great."

He waved as he walked to the restaurant as she jogged Captain around the back to the apartment. She dropped the leash once they reached the stairs.

When Captain reached the top of the steps, he sat in front of the door, a trick Jack had taught him. Another reason Jack pushed the idea of her moving into his place — Captain would have more space. The yard alone made Jack's place a much better option. Maybe she was being stubborn by staying in the apartment. Maybe Jack was really Rachael's knight in shining armor. She might actually have the fairytale. She might actually have a home with someone who loved her.

As Jack shuffled through the paperwork that piled his desk, Alex Martinez stepped into his office.

"Hey, man." Jack hadn't expected him to come by. He stood up and shook his hand while patting him on the shoulder.

"How's it going?" Alex asked. In full uniform, Alex took a seat in front of Jack's desk.

"Good, you?"

"Good. I haven't seen you in a while."

Jack leaned back, swiveling in his chair. "I know, busy."

"How's the new girl in town?" Alex winked.

He moaned, realizing that everyone knew about Rachael and him by this point. Why was he surprised? He changed the subject. "Did you stop by for a visit?"

"The town can't stop talking about this woman." Undeterred, Alex crossed his legs, getting comfortable. "I wondered if you figured out *her* story?"

Jack didn't want to lie to his best friend, but he finally had

Rachael's trust. He had come this far, he didn't want to ruin anything they had.

"Bad breakup, I guess," Jack answered. "Guess he was a real jerk."

Alex shifted his posture, sitting straighter. "Well, I kind of started poking around, and I found out some information."

Jack's heart raced.

"Rachael Hawkins is really Rachael Milano, and married to a cop." Alex's forehead creased.

Jack leaned forward, closer to his friend, looking him in the eye. "She's not hiding anything. She's just came out of a rough relationship."

Alex's leg shook. "Are you sure that's all there is with her?"

"You should probably just drop it," Jack said to him his tone on the edge.

Alex made a face. "Weren't you the one who asked me to look into her?"

The door suddenly opened and Rachael said, "You did what?"

Rachael couldn't believe what she was hearing. He'd had a cop check her out. Before she could stop herself, she pushed through the slightly opened door and both Jack and the officer stood up.

Jack's face turned white. "Rachael."

The officer reached out his hand, but she kept her eye on his gun. "Hello, Rachael, I'm Alex, Jack's friend."

Her heart started racing, pounding through her chest. "You asked him to look into me?"

Jack knew it didn't matter, but he said, "I asked before."

"Why didn't you tell me?"

He looked at Alex, who held up his hands.

"Because I didn't want you to worry."

Jack walked around the desk, but she backed away from him into hall, not exactly sure what to do next. The police officer certainly was suspicious. It would only be a matter of time before he connected the dots.

"Alex is my closest friend, you can trust him."

She just shook her head, unable to look at him. "I can't believe you went behind my back like that."

"I should've told you. I never meant to hurt you."

He reached out to grab her hand, but she pulled it out of his grasp. "Don't."

Her heart tore inside her, like a muscle ripping off a bone.

"Rachael, please."

She turned and ran out, up the stairs and slammed the apartment door. She heard his footsteps behind her, but she tore down the shade. Captain jolted from a deep sleep on the couch.

Jack knocked on the door. Pacing back and forth, she swung open the door. "How could you go to the police?" Her hands went to her forehead. She looked around at the room. The home she thought was real was suddenly becoming another memory.

"Rachael, I promise, I only wanted to help you," he pleaded.

Tears stung at his naivety, and she let out a huff.

Her throat closed up as she spoke. "He probably called Providence."

"Look, I didn't tell him anything other than that you seemed like you were in trouble."

She shook her head, and turned away from him. "You should go," she said, walking toward the bathroom. She couldn't look at him. She no longer trusted him.

CHAPTER 20

*R*achael waited inside her apartment for Jack's friend to come upstairs and arrest her, but when she saw him leave the restaurant and get back into his police vehicle, he didn't even look back. She wondered how much he really knew. How long she had until Nick showed up.

If he dug around enough and called around about her, it would only be a matter of time before Nick found out about it. He probably had tabs on all the police stations in the area. If Jack's friend even called about a strange woman in town, Nick would hear about it. How long ago was that?

She looked around the apartment. Jack's things intermingled with hers. A sweatshirt draped over the kitchen chair, his Red Sox hat by the door. It had felt like a home, if only for that short moment. It felt perfect.

How could he have gone to the police?

Her phone continued to vibrate against the table. Jack hadn't stopped texting since she asked him to leave, but she didn't even look at them. She needed to think about what she had to do next, and she couldn't involve Jack any longer. That, she knew for sure.

Rachael gathered her things together, walking around the space, collecting anything she could take with her. Captain followed at her heels, sitting next to her whenever she stopped. Every once in a while, he'd rest his head against her leg, reminding her of his presence. Not that she forgot. Captain looked up at her, his big brown eyes digging into her soul. How could she leave him behind? Or Finn? Or even Jack?

Adam had filed for divorce, and promised her location would be protected in the documents, but he didn't know Nick like she did. He was a great detective.

She grabbed her bag before leaving a bowl full of kibble on the floor. She left and walked down Harbor Lane. She didn't turn back, even after Jack called her name, afraid she'd change her mind and make things worse.

When she reached the police station, she looked up at the two-story building. The afternoon sun had begun to set, and the windows reflected the golden rays. Her heart raced. This was the only way. She let out a deep breath and opened the glass doors.

In the lobby, a woman in uniform sat behind a tall counter. She looked up as Rachael approached and asked, "Can I help you?"

"Yes, I'd like to speak to Officer Martinez."

Jack sat at his kitchen table and looked out at the water. How did he mess up again? His knee bounced as he rethought everything he had done wrong. Why hadn't he just told Rachael? He could have told her that night at Maggie's. Confessed everything. She would have been upset, but maybe he wouldn't have ruined everything by hiding it from her.

The sound of tires crunching on the gravel caught his attention. Matt's truck pulled up outside.

"Wow, he's back," Matt said, as he walked into the house, closing the door to the garage. He dropped his fishing gear on the floor in the mud room, next to the washer. "You can start my laundry any time."

Jack didn't even bother to acknowledge him, just stared out the window.

Matt walked over to the kitchen table and peered out. "What are we looking at?"

"Nothing."

"Are you sure?"

Jack stood up, stepping closer to the sliding doors. "I messed up with Rachael and I'm not sure if I can fix it."

Matt made a face. "What'd you do?"

Jack leaned against the glass. If he strained, he could just make out the restaurant. The sun reflected in his eyes and he stepped back.

"I kept something from her."

"That certainly doesn't ever work out." Matt took another drink. "Did you apologize?"

Jack shot him a look. "Of course, I did."

"How bad is it?"

"I asked Alex to look into her."

"You did what?" Matt's jaw fell. "Why did you do that?"

"I thought she was in trouble." Jack sat down and put his head between his hands, squeezing his head with his fingers. "She doesn't want to see me. She won't answer my texts."

Matt pulled out the chair next to him and joined him at the table. He nodded as though contemplating the situation. "Maybe you need to apologize again. Sitting here, staring out the window, isn't going to make things better."

Jack looked back out to the afternoon sky. Matt was right, of course, but what more could he say? He messed up. How could he ever gain Rachael's trust again?

"It's way more complicated than that."

"Doesn't seem that complicated." Matt shrugged. "Just as long as I don't have to move again."

～

Rachael stepped into Officer Martinez's office.

"Please, sit."

She folded her hands in her lap, squeezing them tightly when she noticed they were shaking. At this point, especially because of Jack, she was done running.

Officer Martinez leaned forward on his desk. "How can I help you?"

Rachael got right to the point. "Have you talked to my husband?"

The officer shook his head. He pulled out a piece of paper from his desk drawer and handed it over to her. She saw her driver's license photo staring back at her. It was like looking back at a stranger. She looked so old, all the weight of the world resting on her shoulders.

"Have you tried leaving your husband before?" he asked. "Under special circumstances, you can get help from the state."

She looked at him, surprised. Did the officer understand her situation?

"Jack came to me about a new woman in town with a black eye," Officer Martinez said.

She didn't say anything. She wanted to keep Jack out of this.

She looked back down at the photo, then passed it back to him. He picked it up and said, "I had to wonder what would make someone want to change their identity." He passed another piece of paper across the desk, a photograph of Nick from the Providence Police website. "So, he's your husband?"

She nodded as her heart skipped a beat.

"Does he know I'm here?" she asked, her eyes widening as she spoke. The realization that Nick could be anywhere filled her with fear.

He shook his head, but her hands shook as she picked up the paper with his photograph, her stomach twisting as she looked back at Nick's face.

"Look, I…" She didn't know what to say at this point.

Alex stopped her. "You know we have judges here in Maine

that would be more than willing to help a woman leave her abusive husband, even if he is a cop."

Rachael looked at the officer. "If he finds me, I think I'll need more than a judge's restraining order."

She thought of her apartment. Had he come to find her? Did he already know where she was? If this officer figured it all out, Nick would, too.

Alex started talking as her mind raced. "Filing a restraining order is the first thing we can do."

Her mind wandered as he kept talking about the next steps. How he could send a patrol car around to keep an eye out for any suspicious behavior.

"What can you tell me about your husband?" he asked.

"He wants to be the one who finds me."

CHAPTER 21

*J*ack waited inside the restaurant for Rachael to come back home. He had looked everywhere — the Tavern, Finn's place, even called Maggie, but he knew she wasn't far, with Captain still upstairs. He sat in front of the computer looking up at the man who was married to Rachael. Officer Nick Milano, Chief Deputy of Providence Police Department.

The man's cold, gray eyes looked back at Jack. He wanted so badly to punch in the station's number. To hear Nick's voice and warn him to stay away from Rachael. But Jack had no idea what the man was capable of. He didn't want to make the situation worse for her, not knowing what he might do.

Jack searched everything he could about Nick. He dug through all the images and newspaper articles he had been referenced in. The police officer was a local hero. There were no stories about him beating his wife. Instead, there were images of him receiving awards, shaking hands with prominent figures of Providence, and attending special events in full uniform. There were articles with him speaking about a crime he solved, or a criminal he brought to justice. Then, Jack stumbled upon a photo of Nick receiving an award at his local high school. Rachael stood beside him, smiling at the camera.

She looked beautiful, in a pink dress and heels. They look like the perfect couple, but the strange thing was, she didn't look like the Rachael Jack knew. The person who smiled next to Nick Milano looked like a stranger. His jaw tensed.

He looked out the window again. The moon already hung in the afternoon sky. The sun would soon disappear behind the tree line. He wanted Rachael to come back. He didn't want her to be out in the dark, alone.

His eyes were focusing on Nick's face again when he noticed a Camden Cove police cruiser drive down the street and park in front of the restaurant. Alex stepped out, and then so did Rachael. She looked directly into the window and saw him. He watched her from the window as she went up to her apartment with Alex. The two talked, and then he saw her shake his hand.

Jack's heart raced as he watched her step inside.

Matt was right. He needed to apologize again.

"Would you like me to keep an eye on the place?" Officer Martinez asked. "I can have whoever's patrolling swing by every few hours."

Rachael nodded, noticing Jack in the window.

"He was in Providence when I called today," said Alex, trying to reassure her, but it didn't matter where Nick was last seen. Rachael knew he could show up anywhere, at any time.

"That would be great." Rachael reached out her hand to him. "Thank you for everything."

"It's my job." He shook her hand. "I'll start the paperwork and set up a date with a judge."

"Will you make sure to reach out if you hear anything?" she said, hoping to trust the man Jack promised she could.

"I'll come straight to your apartment to tell you in person," Alex said.

He nodded and stepped down the stairs two at a time, then suddenly stopped. He turned back as she unlocked the doors. "Can you do me a favor?"

She nodded. "Sure."

"Don't be mad at Jack." He gestured his head toward the restaurant. "His intentions were good."

She let out a long breath. "I know."

As if he heard them talking about him, Jack stepped out the restaurant's back door. Alex smiled at her and patted Jack on the back. "I'm going to head back to the station and make those calls."

"Thank you," Rachael said again, but her attention on Jack.

"Hey," he said, climbing a stair, looking up at her.

"Hey."

He looked terrible. "I am so, so sorry."

She let out a deep sigh. "You were right. I could trust him."

Jack shook his head. "I shouldn't have overstepped."

"No, you shouldn't have."

"I should have told you at Maggie's place." He climbed up a step.

"Yes, you should have." She went down one.

"Will you ever forgive me?" He climbed up two more.

She reached out to take his hand. "No more secrets."

"No more secrets."

She grabbed his chef's jacket and pulled him close to her. He slid his hands behind her neck, his thumbs resting on her jaw as he leaned over and kissed her. Her arms wrapped around his waist just as Captain jumped up against the door, barking at them. He nestled his face down along her neck as she spoke. "We need to take Captain out, before he breaks out."

He moaned as he looked back at Captain, who stood almost at eye level in the door's window with his tongue hanging out, smiling at them.

"I swear he knows what he's doing," he said, making her laugh.

Captain barked as if he understood what they were saying. She laughed harder as he started licking the window.

Jack leaned over and kissed her again. "Let's take him for a walk."

Rachael kissed him back, her heart swelling inside her chest. "That sounds perfect."

$\sim$

Colleen Connolly hadn't planned to be at Finn's Tavern by herself in the middle of the afternoon, but after she closed on her second vacation home in one week, she thought she'd take her assistant out for a quick drink to celebrate. Soon, Betsy finished her glass of chardonnay and headed home to her fiancé. Colleen ordered another drink and moved to the bar.

She had grown up in Camden Cove, married her first husband right out of high school and divorced here, too. Never could get a handle on another man. Just as well, she thought as a man with smoldering gray eyes looked over at her from the other side of the tavern. She didn't necessarily need a man hanging around all the time, which was why she picked her glass up and walked over to his table. Colleen Connolly was anything but shy, especially around men.

She sauntered over, swinging her hips a little more than usual. Then she used her best line on him. "You must be new in town, are you here for business?"

She learned early on that men loved to talk about themselves. She could tell he was rolling what he was about to say around in his head. Then, just as she expected, he was hooked. "Actually, I'm looking for a woman."

"Well, you've found her."

He pulled out a brown leather wallet and flipped it open. A gold police badge shone in the light. It made her like him even more.

"How can I help you, officer?" She slanted her eyes at his

name. Without her reading glasses, she could barely make out the letters. "Officer Milano?"

He pulled out a photograph from inside his jacket pocket, handing it over to her, and she recognized the pretty face right away. "I told people she'd be trouble."

The man smiled. "So, you've run into her?"

She nodded. "Yes, pretty young thing. Came into town with a pretty big black eye, too."

He nodded, but looked around the bar and not at Colleen, which bothered her. "Do you know if she still works here?"

Colleen wondered what kind of trouble the girl was in. "Well, I don't see her here much anymore, but she has been hanging around The Fish Market with Jack Williams."

He plucked the photo from her fingers and put it back into his coat pocket. He threw a twenty on the table and stood up. He nodded at Colleen, who slowly realized her night was coming to a quick end.

"If you see her again, give me a call." He threw a card out from his wallet.

"What if I called about something else?" she said, hoping he'd forget about police work for a few hours.

"Just if you see her," he said back, his tone harsh, and she instantly disliked him.

As he walked away from the table, she picked up the card and stuffed it into her pocket. She downed the rest of her wine and then said goodnight to the young bartender with a wink.

Stepping out of the tavern, the chilly evening air greeted her and she noticed a car off in the distance with out-of-state plates. Which state, she couldn't determine from where she stood, but she figured it was the nitwit officer. She turned around and tossed his card into a trash can as she walked away.

CHAPTER 22

The sun had just peeked above the horizon, casting a pink glow throughout the apartment as Jack came inside. The smell of coffee hit him. On the counter, a travel mug sat all ready for him.

"Good morning," she said, kissing him. "You ready for a walk, Cap?"

The dog jumped against the door the second Rachael said it.

"Hold on," Jack said, pulling him off the door and settling him down into a sitting position.

"Are you sure you want to take him? It's freezing." Rachael asked.

He looked out at the cold air, now regretting offering to take Captain for a walk. Subarctic weather had blown into town.

The idea of crawling under a warm blanket with her instead sounded perfect. Then Captain barked at him.

"I'll just go up the trail and head back." He pulled his hood over his hat, pulling his gloves on. "It'll be fine."

"Do you think you'll be long?" she looked out at the trail. He could tell she was calculating times. She said she was fine, but since she had come back, she no longer wanted to be alone without Captain or him. The first sign of her anxiety was the lights. She always had them on. At night, she frequently wanted him to sleep on the couch and the nights he did go home, she made him promise to come back early in the morning for their walk. "I think I'll go to the bakery while you're gone."

"We'll walk you there," he said, her face filling with relief.

He promised himself, if there was one thing he would do for Rachael, it was to make her feel safe again.

As Rachael sat at the window in the bakery and sipped her coffee, she watched the goings-on of the now familiar town. With Frank's recommendation, she chose a chocolate choux bun pastry. The cream filling and the generous coat of melted dark chocolate blended together in her mouth, and she polished it off in three bites. Frank brought another pastry when he sat down with her as the crowd dwindled.

"What do you think, now that you've stayed awhile?" Frank asked.

She looked out at the harbor. Lobster boats dipped in the water, bouncing up and down along the surface. The shop fronts along the waterfront looked like something out of a postcard, not her back yard. Beyond, the wide-open water spread out before her as far as the eye could see. "I never want to leave."

"Well, I hope it becomes home for you," he said, suddenly distracted as another customer walked in the door. He stood up and grabbed her empty plate before heading back to the counter.

She thought about Finn and Sunday dinner. She'd ask Finn if she could invite Jack, although, she knew he'd say yes. He liked Jack just as much as she did.

After she finished her coffee, she walked the mug over to the counter and handed it to Frank. "Have a nice day."

"You know where to find us if you need anything," Frank said.

"Will you tell Jack I headed home?"

"Of course," he said, kissing her on the cheek.

She walked down Harbor Lane toward the restaurant, keeping an eye out for Jack and Captain. He said he wouldn't be long, but now with the sun out, it felt warmer, he might keep their routine, which was to walk to Perkin's beach and back.

When she reached the apartment and opened the door, she decided it was time to call her mom. Tell her about things, about Jack. Officer Martinez called her the night before to tell her that he had filed for a petition. It was up to the judge at this point, but Adam said the district attorney gave him the impression it wouldn't be a problem to file for divorce even if Nick hadn't responded.

Now all she had to do was wait.

As she stepped inside, she half expected to see Jack and Captain already there, but she walked into a dark apartment, all the shades drawn and the lights off. Then she noticed the bathroom door was closed. Her heart dropped.

Her legs froze, her muscles immediately tensing up. She was about to turn around and leave, when she saw a shadowed figure shut the door behind her and before she could react, a blow to her head made a bright white explosion, and she was on the floor before she knew what was happening. The pain blasted through her head and down the side of her face. Her vision blurred as she tried to get up. She looked at a figure, but it was hard to distinguish his features. She couldn't hear what he was saying over the sharp ringing in her ears.

Her hands patted the floor, trying to get enough friction to pull herself up, but the pain made her dizzy and she fell again, hitting her head against the wooden floors.

"How could you leave me?" His voice sounded slurred and low. She blinked hard, trying to focus on his face, but couldn't steady her vision. He grabbed her arm and pulled her up, throwing her into the chair next to the couch. "How could you run away from me and leave me for dead?"

A metallic taste filled her mouth and slowly she focused in on his face.

His lips snarled as he spoke. "I should've killed you that night."

She jumped up out of the chair but he threw her back, pulling out his gun.

He grabbed her with both hands, his gun pressing against her face as he screamed at her. "You think you can live without me?!"

She jerked her head, but his grip was too tight. He straddled her, holding her down, and pressed his lips against hers as she wrestled with every part of her body to get out of his grasp, but it was no use. He pressed the barrel of the gun against her forehead.

"It's time for you to come home, Rachael."

Jack walked along the trail with Captain, holding a handful of dog food as he practiced commands with him. He was a scatter-brain of a dog, sniffing one thing, then forgetting what he was doing and moving onto another, but he was a good boy. And once he had a few training classes, Captain would make a fine dog.

Seagulls flew above them in the late morning breeze, reminding him how he wanted to take Rachael on a real picnic in Camden Cove. Maybe instead of going to Maggie's, they could sit on the beach and let Captain run around. They'd have the whole place to themselves at this time of year.

When he swung by the bakery, Frank said, "You just missed Rachael."

"I was hoping to grab a few treats." He decided to go directly to the source. His uncles couldn't resist being part of things.

"Treats for what?"

"I'd like to take Rachael on a picnic."

Frank winked at him. "Do you even have to ask?" He called through the window to the kitchen. "David, we need to whip up some warm finger foods for a picnic!"

"Who's going on a picnic on a day like today?" David poked his head out. "Oh, it's you, Jack."

Jack suddenly felt like a teenager again. "I wanted to take Rachael to Perkin's beach."

"At this time of year? We'll definitely have to pack a thermos of hot cocoa."

"So, we were right about the picnic," Frank said, raising an eyebrow.

Jack made a face. "You were right."

Frank filled a box with chocolate croissants, fruit tarts, and two cups. "Make sure you bring a warm blanket."

"You should really do it at night and have a campfire," David said from behind the counter.

Frank's eyes lit up. "Right at that tiny cove by your place. It's a perfect spot. With the rocks on either side of you, it'll block out the wind."

Jack thought of the cove. It was where he first saw her with Captain. He looked down at the dog, who sat happily at his feet.

This time he didn't question his uncles. "That sounds perfect, actually."

Jack left the bakery with a new zest in his step as he walked along the sidewalk. He had pulled out his phone to call the fire department about a fire permit, when he noticed the light above the apartment's door had been turned off. Had Rachael turned off another light?

He smiled to himself. Maybe she was doing better today.

Captain tugged ahead toward the restaurant, but Jack pulled him back as he looked for the department's number on his phone. "No tugging, Cap."

He checked the department's website as Captain growled deep in his throat, then out of nowhere tried to run toward the steps to the apartment.

"What is it, Cap?" Jack looked for the squirrel that stole the dog's attention. He tried to pull Captain back, but the dog was at full alert. The hair on his back stood up and he used all his weight to pull the leash, strangling himself. "Chill out, Captain."

Jack stuffed his phone in his pocket, using both hands to pull the dog back. Captain barked, jumping toward the stairs, twisting his body to get out of his collar. Jack had never seen him act like this. Then he saw the door without the light on. He jogged up the steps, turned the knob, and realized it was locked. Obviously, Rachael still had her fears, but this was different.

He knocked, holding Captain down from scratching up the door. He peeked inside, not hearing anything. "Rachael?"

He knocked again. "Rachael?"

Pulling out his phone, he checked to see if he had missed a message. Did she leave? Or maybe she was in the bathroom. He looked inside again, blocking out the sun's reflection with his hands. The apartment looked empty.

He pulled out his set of keys, flipping through all the different tinges of silver and brass shapes until he found the right one and slipped it into the keyhole. He hoped she wouldn't be upset for going inside. He just couldn't shake the feeling something was off. Captain scratched at the door as he turned the knob and pushed open the door. He let go of the leash just as he stepped inside.

He didn't hear the pops until after he felt the burn in his shoulder. The basket dropped from his hand, spilling the contents all over the floor. The jolt threw him back against the doorframe and he was only vaguely aware of a man yelling. He could just make out Rachael from the other side of the apartment. Captain jumped up and bit the man, ripping at his arm. More shots rang out, and then a yelp.

Jack struggled to pull himself up, his shoulder on fire, his arm not moving no matter how hard he tried. Rachael had escaped the man's grip and leaped across the floor toward the gun, but Nick grabbed hold of her.

Jack gained momentum and pulled himself up, his legs

wobbling. He pounded his left fist as hard as he could into the back of Nick's head. Nick stumbled, but swung back at Jack's face. Stars flashed in his eyes. He pounded Nick's jaw with his knuckles, but fell back into the table as Nick reached for his throat, squeezing with both hands.

"Get out of here!" Jack coughed out at Rachael, though his words were barely audible. "Go!"

His vision turned black around the edges as he wrestled in Nick's grasp, but he saw Rachael moving. *Keep going* he thought, as Nick's grip tightened. His breath completely cut off.

"Let him go." Her voice was steady, but the gun shook in her hands.

Nick's clutch didn't loosen. He only tightened it around Jack's neck. But Nick focused his attention on Rachael and the gun, and it gave Jack the distraction he needed to crack his forehead into Nick's, sending him backwards, losing his grip. Jack fell against the table, gasping for breath, splinters of pain racing through his throat.

Nick held up his hands as he walked toward Rachael. His arm was bleeding. "Rachael, don't do anything stupid."

Jack struggled to his feet, grabbing the edge of the table. He stumbled toward the counter as Rachael cocked the gun.

Nick moved closer as she kept the gun on him. "Killing a cop would be the end for you."

Jack slipped as he reached the counter and tried to pull himself up from the floor, reaching for anything he could grab. Off in the distance he heard the howling of sirens, but he knew it'd be too late. Nick rushed at Rachael, but Jack swung the bat, falling to the ground with Nick, their bodies pounding against the floor. The ringing in his ears made Rachael's voice echo. He coughed and turned onto his stomach. He could see her feet as she ran to him, pulling him up into her lap. He coughed harder, the words he wanted to speak burning in his throat.

"Get out of here." He leaned over, crying out in pain. "You need to get out of here."

Rachael shook her head, the gun trembling in her hand. "I'm not leaving you or Captain."

She held the gun on Nick as she helped Jack to his feet. The pain took Jack's breath away, and before he could focus on her, everything went black.

CHAPTER 23

*E*verything happened in a blur. Rachael hardly remembered when Officer Martinez took the gun out of her hand while the paramedics tended to Jack, pulling him out of her lap and onto a stretcher. Another paramedic put pressure on Jack's shoulder. He went in and out of consciousness for a few minutes, frightening her.

By the time they brought Jack to the ambulance, he was responding, but couldn't move.

"Make sure she's okay," he said, without opening his eyes.

"I'm fine, you worry about you." She didn't move from Jack's side, not letting go of him even as they lifted him inside.

"I want the dog to come, too," Jack demanded.

When the paramedic began to argue with Jack, Alex lifted Captain into his own arms. "I'll bring him to Elizabeth right now."

Captain licked Alex's face as he hoisted him up and put him in the back seat of his police cruiser. She didn't even notice that Nick had been rushed out by ambulance until the sirens flashed by them. She kept her focus on Jack who smiled at her, even as the paramedics worked on his shoulder. He'd wince, then give her a smile, then winced again.

"He's going to be okay, right?" she asked the paramedic.

"Ma'am you're going to have to let go," the man said as he taped the IV to Jack's arm.

"I'm going with him," she said.

The man made a face, then pointed to a seat against the wall. "You should be in your own ambulance."

The two paramedics applied pressure on his chest, and Jack let out a deep groan.

"You guys need to make sure she's okay," Jack moaned out. "She was hit pretty bad along the side of her face."

"We will, sir, now just stay still."

"He's going to be okay," another man said, reassuring her as he got into the driver's seat, turning the sirens on. Just as they pulled away, Frank and David ran down Harbor Lane and saw her in the vehicle.

"You better call them and tell them I'm okay. God knows how quickly this news will spread." Jack groaned again as the paramedics cut open his shirt.

"Stop worrying about everyone else, and stop talking," the woman paramedic ordered.

Rachael looked back again and saw him looking up at her. He mouthed the words, *I love you.*

"I love you, too."

It didn't take long for the whole Williams clan to show up at the hospital. Even Lauren drove from Boston in record-breaking time.

"You had to have been going over ninety miles an hour," Jack said.

"I was worried!" She leaned over and hugged him.

"Ah," he growled through his clenched jaw. "That's my bad side."

"Oh, sorry."

Rachael sat next to him in a chair beside the bed. She had seven stitches along her forehead and a concussion, but the doctors told him she'd be fine with some rest.

"I can't believe you wanted to keep the bullet." Elizabeth shook her head as Matt held up the plastic evidence bag his hand.

Sarah sat on Jack's other side, with John rubbing her shoulders. "It could have been much worse."

"What about Nick?" Matt asked.

"He's already been charged and placed in Portland," Alex said, taking the bullet back from Matt and stuffing it into his chest pocket.

"I talked to the judge about getting Rachael's medical records sent up from Providence as soon as possible, which will help corroborate her story."

"He's not getting out, is he?" Finn asked.

Jack could feel his heart rate rising.

Alex shook his head. "No, they'll hold him at least until they process his court date, but with him being a danger to society, I have a feeling they'll keep him in custody."

Matt crossed his arms and said, "What I'm most surprised about is how much that dog likes you. I mean, to attack Nick like he did. He practically ripped his arm off."

"Captain was really only protecting *Rachael*," Elizabeth teased.

Jack rolled his eyes. "You guys are busting on me even as I lie shot-up in a hospital bed."

"You're fine. It was only in your shoulder. No vital organs were hurt." Elizabeth said, but she leaned over on his good side, hugged him and didn't let go.

When everyone left the room and the doctors told all the family to go home, Jack made Rachael promise to stay. She lay down beside him on the hospital bed, watching him as he slept. She gently traced his jaw with her fingertips and smelled his scent for the hundredth time. She had never believed in miracles, or angels, or luck, but the moment Jack came up to her the night she arrived in Camden Cove was the luckiest moment of her life.

As the night wore on, nurses came in and out, ignoring that Rachael had broken the visiting hours rule, and did their thing around them. Each time, Rachael asked what next needed to be done for Jack's care. She stayed awake all night, making sure everything was alright, even though the nurses told her she needed just as much rest with a concussion. She didn't care. She wanted to make sure he was okay.

From beside her, Jack moaned suddenly and grabbed his shoulder.

She jumped up, ready to call the nurses. "Do you need more medicine? Do you want me to call the doctor?"

He shushed her, placing his finger on her lips, his eyes still closed. With his good arm, he reached out to her and gently pulled her back into her former position at his side. "Now I'm good."

He rubbed her back, and she could tell he was falling back to sleep.

"Thank you, Jack," she whispered into his ear.

"No problem." He let out a deep breath, his hand continuing to rub.

She looked up at him, tears forming in the corners of her eyes. "I don't know what I would've done if something worse had happened to you."

He shushed her again, then looked down at her. "I needed you to learn to trust me, somehow."

She laughed at his bad joke, leaned over and kissed him. "I love you."

"I love you, too." He closed his eyes again.

And when Jack fell asleep, she made a promise to take care of him for the rest of her life.

CHAPTER 24

*J*ack stayed two nights in the hospital and was finally discharged in the afternoon. Sarah fussed around him, asking a hundred questions, making sure all his vitals were okay, and annoyed the doctor about his prescriptions. Rachael sat next to him, watching and listening to it all. They wheeled Jack out to Matt's truck and all rode to Jack's together.

"126 Seaside Drive," Matt said as he pulled into the driveway. "You've arrived."

The sling pressed against his stomach, making him uncomfortable. He adjusted it, letting out a moan, and Matt slowly came to a very long stop. "Are you okay?"

"Just park."

Jack rolled his eyes, wincing as he tried to grab the door.

"Let Rachael help you," Sarah said as she got out of the truck.

Rachael gave him her new look. The one that said, *let me do it.*

She leaned over and pushed the door open for him, but before he got out, while they were alone for just a second, he kissed her.

Pride filled him as his family and Rachael fretted after him as he walked up to his house. It was as if everything he had ever worked for up until that moment was all worth it. And someday, he wanted nothing more than to give Rachael a beautiful home, a place where she could feel safe and loved, where some day they could raise a family and grow old together.

Elizabeth opened the front door and Captain came hobbling out, barking at Jack and Rachael. He took his time, but made it to them.

"Hey, Cap." Jack bent down and opened up his free arm as Captain made his way to him. He embraced Captain's neck and hugged him. "Thanks a lot, buddy."

Rachael teared up as Captain licked Jack's face, his tail wagging.

"He's going to heal faster than you," Elizabeth said. "Only got nicked by the gunshot in his back." She pointed to the shaven spot on his rear end.

Jack walked Rachael to the front door. He kissed her on the cheek as he opened the door, then waved his hand for her to enter. "I'd pick you up..." he made a face at his arm, "but you'd probably do better carrying me."

She laughed, but hugged him, making him wince.

"Oh, sorry!"

"It's fine, I'm fine."

He opened the door to the small cottage. He had done quite a bit of work to make the house work for him, but now he worried if it would work for her someday. She walked through into the kitchen, which sat in the back of the house. It was his favorite spot. He imagined sitting in the mornings as the sun rose above the water with a cup of coffee, his hand in Rachael's.

"It's a beautiful house." She spun around and faced him.

He couldn't wait to get everyone out of there.

They all congregated in the kitchen and ate the seafood lasagna the restaurant had prepared, a plate of pastries provided by Frank and David, and a twelve pack of Finn's favorite pale ale. The whole family told embarrassing stories of Jack. Elizabeth told of the time he had broken his collarbone playing football and acted dramatically about his injury, warning Rachael of what she'd face in upcoming days. Sarah laid out all his medication and wrote notes on a pad of paper, reminding Rachael that he needed to take them every six hours.

Elizabeth suggested everyone give Jack time to rest, hugging Rachael on the way out. Shortly after, everyone else left, leaving Jack and Rachael standing in the middle of the living room. He pressed a playlist on his phone, and music started to play in the background. He grabbed her hand and walked her to the space between the kitchen and the living room. Captain lay on the mat in front of the sink. He pressed another button and the fireplace whooshed on, illuminating the room with a warm glow. Her laugh bubbled out as he drew her close to him, pressing her against his chest and beginning to dance. Swaying to the music and humming along, she rested her head upon his chest and followed his lead.

"Your uncles wanted me to tell you there's a basket in the fridge" Her left eyebrow lifted up. "What are you all up to?"

He shrugged glad he could count on them. He had texted them earlier asking for another picnic.

"Thought we could go on a picnic."

Captain led them down the trail as Rachael carried the basket in one arm and a couple of blankets in the other. The winter afternoon held a chill, but it didn't bother her as they walked down to the beach.

"Watch it." Rachael nervously grabbed hold of Jack's coat as he climbed down the side of the cliff, using his good hand to guide him, but he didn't need help. It looked like he could climb down the rock ledge with his eyes closed. Captain, half-skipped, half-waddled down to the cove's beach. With the tide out, the waves lapped against the sand, making a soft hushing sound off in the distance as the seagulls glided above them in the wind.

Inside the cove, a stack of firewood sat perfectly, ready for a match. "How did you do this?"

Jack smiled. "I have my ways."

Rachael spread out the blanket on top of two logs next to the fire pit and placed the basket on top, about to sit, but Jack grabbed her hand and pulled her toward the water. "Come with me."

They walked out to the water's edge as Captain chased the waves rolling to shore. Jack stopped and held her in his arms, facing the granite cliffs, the house beyond and the town off to the side. The afternoon sun sat on top of the trees, falling behind the bare branches. She noticed all the lights were turned on in the house, even the lights outside in the yard. It was the most beautiful house she had ever seen.

She looked back at him, and that's when he knelt down. He held a ring in his fingertips.

"I know you aren't even technically divorced, but I want to make you happy for the rest of your life."

He held out a thin gold band with a shining round diamond. She reached out and took it. It was the most beautiful ring she had ever seen.

"It was my grandmother's, but we can get you something else, if you'd like."

"It's perfect."

He leaned down. "So? Will you make me the happiest man on earth, and spend the rest of my life with me?"

She wrapped her arms around Jack's neck, as the seagulls soared above them and kissed him. "Yes."

∾

I hope you enjoyed *The Restaurant by the Cove*! The next book in the series, *The Christmas Cottage by the Cove*, focuses on Kate and Matt, who reunite for a Christmas miracle after Kate's fiancé leaves her just before the holidays. Click HERE to start reading *The Christmas Cottage by the Cove*.

. . .

Click HERE for a FREE copy of *The Wedding by the Cove,* which is only available to newsletter subscribers. This novella takes you to Zoe and Ethan's wedding, where new love blossoms between Amelia and Ryan! Besides the free story, newsletter subscribers also receive special offers and updates on new releases.

Click HERE or visit ellenjoyauthor.com for more information about Ellen Joy's other books.

<u>Cliffside Point</u>
Beach Home Beginnings
Seaview Cottage
Sugar Beach Sunsets
Home on the Harbor
Christmas at Cliffside
Lakeside Lighthouse
Seagrass Sunrise
Half Moon Harbor
Seashell Summer
Beach Home Dreams

<u>Camden Cove</u>
The Inn by the Cove
The Farmhouse by the Cove
The Restaurant by the Cove
The Christmas Cottage by the Cove
The Bakery by the Cove

<u>Prairie Valley Sisters</u>
Coming Home to the Valley
Daydreams in the Valley
Starting Over in the Valley
Second Chances in the Valley
New Hopes in the Valley
Feeling Blessed in the Valley

<u>Blueberry Bay</u>
The Cottage on Blueberry Bay
The Market on Blueberry Bay

Beach Rose Secrets

ACKNOWLEDGMENTS

First, I want to thank my men for always being there for me. None of these words would have been written without your support. Thank you. I love you, more!!! Also, a very special thank you to my own Prince Charming. I live the fairy tale.

Thank you to Katie Page for another extraordinary job editing this manuscript. Your sense of a story is wonderful and I have learned so much from you. Thank you for making my books as good as they are, because they wouldn't be without you. Thank you.

Thank to Zoe Book Design. I LOVE my covers!

Thank you to my mom for being the last eyes on the manuscript. Thank you for all that you have done for me!

Thank you Tina Durham-Bars for another wonderful job proofreading my story! You always find something no one else did!

Thank you to Danielle St. Laurent-Thorne. Where do I begin? I don't know how I got so lucky having a friend like you, but seriously, your no hold back approach made this book what it is. Thank you!!! I love our friendship!

Thank you to Darcy Favorite-Brewster. You're badass-ness is contagious. You inspire me to be a warrior. Thank you for being my first reader always.

Thank you to the New Hampshire Romance Writers of America. I hope to one day be all that you are!

Thank you to Salem Police Officer Jeff Ouellette. First, thank you for protecting our schools, but also for helping me with the integrity of the piece.

Thank you to Robyn Eldredge for always being my most

supportive reader! I am so glad our sons met. You've not only been a great friend, vet and reader, but you're one of the greatest ever. Thank you.

Thank you to my parents who taught me the world of reading.

Domestic Abuse is unfortunately a real story. Every nine seconds in the United States, a woman is assaulted or beaten by a loved one. It's also the leading cause of injury to woman, more than car accidents, muggings and rapes combined. And sadly, each day, a woman is killed by her husband or boyfriend. If you or anyone you know is a victim of domestic violence it's never too late to get help. It is available. It might save her life.

The National Domestic Hotline (800) 799-SAFE.

https://www.womenshealth.gov/relationships-and-safe-ty/get-help/how-help-friend

ABOUT THE AUTHOR

Ellen lives in a small town in New England, between the Atlantic Ocean and the White Mountains. She lives with her husband, two sons, and one very spoiled puppy princess.

Ellen writes in the early morning hours before her family wakes up. When she's not writing, you can find her spending time with her family, gardening, or headed to the beach. She loves summer and flip-flops, running on a dirt country road, and a sweet love song.

All of her stories are clean romances where families are close, neighbors are nosy, and the couples are destined for each other.

Made in United States
North Haven, CT
09 September 2024

57181601R00146